Emma and the Ruby Ring

Yvonne MacGrory

Emma and the Ruby Ring

Illustrations by Terry Myler

MILKWEED
EDITIONS

© 2002, Text by Yvonne MacGrory
© 2002, Cover and interior art by Terry Myler
All rights reserved. Except for brief quotations in critical articles or reviews, no part of this book may be reproduced in any manner without prior written permission from the publisher: Milkweed Editions, 1011 Washington Avenue South, Suite 300, Minneapolis, Minnesota 55415.
(800) 520-6455 / www.milkweed.org / www.worldashome.org

Published 2002 by Milkweed Editions
First published as *The Quest of the Ruby Ring* in 1999 by The Children's Press, Dublin, Ireland.
Printed in the United States of America
Cover and interior art by Terry Myler
The text of this book is set in Plantin
02 03 04 05 06   5 4 3 2 1
First U.S. Edition

Special underwriting was provided for this book in honor of
Eric, Ashley, and Adam.

Milkweed Editions, a nonprofit publisher, gratefully acknowledges support for our intermediate fiction from Alliance for Reading funders: Ecolab Foundation; Marshall Field's Project Imagine with support from the Target Foundation; Target Stores; James R. Thorpe Foundation; United Arts Partnership Funds; and West Group. Other support has been provided by Elmer L. and Eleanor J. Andersen Foundation; Bush Foundation; Faegre and Benson Foundation; General Mills Foundation; McKnight Foundation; Minnesota State Arts Board through an appropriation by the Minnesota State Legislature and a grant from the National Endowment for the Arts and a grant from the Wells Fargo Foundation; A Resource for Change technology grant from the National Endowment for the Arts; Lawrence and Elizabeth Ann O'Shaughnessy Charitable Income Trust in honor of Lawrence M. O'Shaughnessy; Oswald Family Foundation; Ritz Foundation on behalf of Mr. and Mrs. E. J. Phelps Jr.; John and Beverly Rollwagen Fund of the Minneapolis Foundation; St. Paul Companies, Inc.; U.S. Bancorp Foundation; and generous individuals.

Library of Congress Cataloging-in-Publication Data

MacGrory, Yvonne.
    Emma and the ruby ring / Yvonne MacGrory ; [illustrations by Terry Myler].—1st ed.
      p. cm.
    Also published under title: The quest of the ruby ring. Ireland : The Children's Press.
    Sequel to: Martha and the ruby ring.
    Summary: A magic ring transports eleven-year-old Emma to nineteenth-century Ireland, where she and two young girls unravel a mystery at Moylough Castle.
    ISBN 1-57131-634-5 (pbk.) — ISBN 1-57131-635-3
    [1. Time travel—Fiction. 2. Ireland—History—19th century—Fiction. 3. Magic—Fiction. 4. Mystery and detective stories.] I. Myler, Terry, ill. II. Title.

PZ7.M174 Em 2002
[Fic]—dc21
                                                    2001044862

This book is printed on acid-free paper.

For my niece
Amanda

Emma and the Ruby Ring

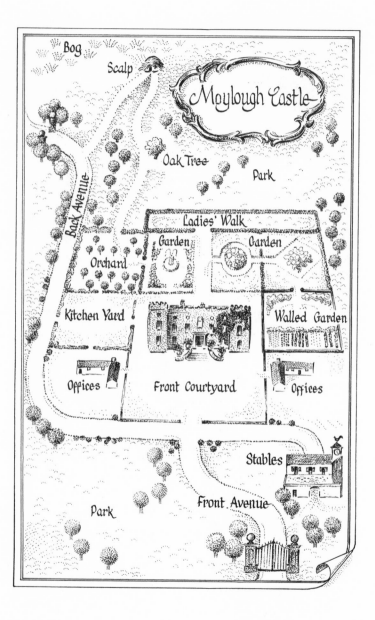

Emma and the Ruby Ring

The Ruby Ring

Standing at the bedroom window, heedless of the hot August sunshine that streamed into the room, Emma Martin's grip on the glazed cotton curtain tightened slightly as she gave another sigh of disappointment.

This should have been the last day of her holidays with the McLaughlins in Donegal. Tomorrow would be her eleventh birthday and it was to have been a special day. She had been looking forward to the drive back to Galway and the stop for lunch on the way. Just she and Dad. Like it had been for a few years since Mum had died. Then Dad had gotten married again. She liked Helen and, seeing Dad's newfound happiness, accepted that the close bond that had grown up between her and her dad would now have to include a third person. But a year ago baby Maeve was born and it seemed to her that Dad didn't have as much time for her. And now this! Her birthday was ruined. Why did things always have to change?

Maeve had been admitted to hospital with suspected meningitis, and Rory Martin had phoned the McLaughlins to say that he would have to remain in Galway until the tests were completed. Could Emma stay for another few days? Emma knew there was nothing else he could have done and she could imagine how worried he and Helen were. But even though she

understood, she couldn't help feeling upset and un-
wanted. Her father hadn't even asked to speak to her.
And surely she could have gone home by herself. . . .

Abruptly she moved away from the window, wishing she had gone swimming with Lucy and David
after all. Now it was too late and the whole long afternoon lay before her. She could have gone downstairs
to join Jean and Paul McLaughlin, who were in the
kitchen, but she felt she wasn't in the mood to talk
to anyone. Resignedly, she decided to get herself a
book—at least reading would pass the time until the
others came home. She went down to the living room
and inspected the bookshelves, eventually settling for
Jane Eyre. On her way back upstairs, the sound of
voices in the kitchen reached her. She heard her name.
They were talking about her.

"I know Emma had it rough when her mother
died, but Rory and Helen have created a wonderful
home for her. I think she's gotten very self-centered,"
Paul was saying.

"You're thinking about yesterday, aren't you? After
old Mrs. Breslin had a fall in the square," said Jean.

"Yes. When the rest of you ran to help, Emma did
nothing. Just stood there, wondering if she would get
back here in time as there was something on TV she
wanted to watch. If that's not total self-absorption,
then I don't know what is."

"I must admit I was rather taken aback myself,"
agreed Jean.

Emma, cheeks on fire, didn't wait to hear any more. She ran upstairs to Lucy's room, which she was sharing, and silently shut the door. She hadn't thought too much about the old lady since yesterday; to be honest, she hadn't thought about her at all. At the time, she had considered that there were plenty of people around who could help. Jean and Lucy and David didn't *have* to rush to the rescue. And just because she hadn't joined in the rush, did that make her selfish and uncaring? But the more she thought about it, the more she realized she never did very much to help anyone, even though she was resentful when other people didn't give her help when she needed it. This thought had never occurred to her before. She resolved to think of others in the future.

And what had Paul called her? Self-centered! That wasn't true. Or was it? Now she remembered that when Lucy had asked her to come swimming she had refused, even though she knew that Lucy and David had arranged to meet some friends at the pool. She also remembered that as she turned away to go upstairs, David had muttered, "No point asking her. She only does what she wants to do!" And it was true that all through the holidays David and Lucy always did what she wanted to do. Then Lucy's whispered reply came to her mind: "Cheer up, she'll soon be going home."

In a somber frame of mind she began to read, but Jane's lonely life at Gateshead Hall with her nasty cousins and her trials at Lowood, the harsh boarding school she was sent to by her cruel aunt, could not hold her attention. Words without meaning danced before her eyes and she had to reread parts to make sense of them. Two large tears splashed onto the page. She stared blearily at the damp circles for a moment before closing the book and going to the dressing table for tissue. The tears were flowing freely now, and as she caught sight of herself in the mirror she groaned aloud. Her blue eyes were puffy and her mouth drooped at the corners—she always looked a mess when she cried. "There, thinking of myself again," she thought. "This will have to stop."

As she dabbed her eyes and tried a smile, a flash of red beneath the mirror caught her eye. Taking a closer look she saw it was Lucy's ruby ring. Lucy sometimes wore it but never when she went swimming. It really was beautiful, thought Emma, as she took it from its small brown box and slipped it on her finger.

A clicking sound made her stop. "I hope I haven't broken the stupid box," she thought nervously. "Lucy will be sure to think I did it on purpose. Not to worry—it's still intact. But what's this?" She looked at the small gold lettering on the back of the box and read aloud:

> The secret of this ruby ring,
> Is that two wishes it can bring . . .

"Secrets, wishes coming true. Kids' stuff!"

As she absentmindedly twisted the ring, she

thought about old Mrs. Breslin. Why hadn't she helped to pick up her parcels or offered to run for the doctor? At least she could have said she would see her home, as Lucy had, when it was decided Mrs. Breslin had no injuries and was only shaken.

"I'm selfish," Emma decided. "Rotten selfish. But I don't really mean to be. If only I had the chance to prove it. To do something for someone and not think about myself for a change. Something really big. Not just picking up parcels, but something that would be the difference between life and death. Like saving someone from a burning building . . . or from drowning. Then Jean and Paul would realize that I'm not self-centered. Thoughtless, maybe. But not selfish."

As she reflected how unlikely it was that she would ever get the chance to act the heroine, she began to feel a little strange. "Why do I feel so odd? My head is spinning. Everything is going blurry. Like flu coming on. Such a peculiar feeling . . ."

The Workhouse

As if in a dream, Emma heard people crying and shouting, and as the sounds got closer and closer she put her hands over her ears to shut out the despairing cries. But there was no escape. She was in the middle of a howling mob. All around her were people dressed in filthy rags, their thin arms stretched beseechingly toward the entrance of a huge gray stone building surrounded by high walls. As the crowd surged around the stout wooden gates, the rain began to fall. Soon everyone was soaked to the skin and the wet tangle of hair, plastered across bony heads, accentuated the gaunt faces and staring eyes of men, women, and children.

Every now and then the gates opened a fraction to admit a few people who passed in bits of paper. Then the gates were quickly closed again.

A cart drew up, and the driver cleared the crowd from the gates. Emma was almost overcome by the stench that rose from the unwashed bodies pressing against her. A woman and two children, one about Emma's age, the other younger with fair hair, got down from the cart. The woman, her face ghastly in color, seemed barely able to stand. Emma thought the woman would surely fall, but the older girl put a supporting arm around her waist as the driver rapped loudly on the gate.

There was a low murmuring from the crowd as someone shouted that the gates were about to open again. The murmuring grew into a torrent of cries and screams and there was a sudden surge as everyone pushed forward. The little fair-haired girl was separated from her companions and shoved roughly aside.

"Maria!" cried the older girl, unable to leave the woman, who now seemed half conscious. "For God's sake, will no one help her?"

Seeing Maria's plight, Emma rushed forward. Grabbing Maria, she shouldered their way through the crowd to join Maria's two companions. On reaching the gate Emma asked breathlessly, "What is this place? What's happening? Why does everyone want to get in? And why won't they let them?"

"This is one of the most crowded workhouses. They'll only take you in if you have papers."

"Papers? What do you mean?"

"You have to have an order signed by a relieving officer."

"What about those who haven't?" asked Emma in alarm.

"They'll have to go back home—if they have a home. Or find someone to take them in—if they're lucky. Though that's not very likely. A lot of them will die by the roadside." The girl looked at Emma as the

driver rapped the gate again. "But you don't look starving. You must have a home. Why don't you go back?"

"I have nowhere to go. My mother is dead. I have no one. Let me come with you. Please," Emma pleaded desperately.

The girl hesitated for a moment. Then as the gate opened a fraction, she relented. "All right then, seeing you were good enough to rescue Maria. Come in behind us. But be quick."

The driver thrust a grubby slip of paper into the porter's hand, and the paper was carefully examined. Apparently satisfied, the porter opened the gate a fraction wider to admit them. With a loud clang it closed behind them.

They were in!

A small courtyard stretched before them. Someone gestured them through the door of the stone building that faced them and a woman curtly told them to join the end of a queue. As the line moved slowly toward three people who were sitting at a table at the head of the room, Emma listened to the shreds of conversations going on around her, shocked to hear such hopelessness in the voices of both men and women. Most of them were like the people she had seen outside the workhouse, their ragged clothes barely covering their emaciated frames.

"We sold our last blanket a few days ago," one woman was saying to anyone who would listen. "They came and pulled our cabin down. Evicted. So the fat landlord in London won't have to pay the rates for us. Everything gone."

A man, shock plain in his voice, whispered, "I don't care what happens to me now. All my family are dead from fever."

"We should have emigrated when we had the chance. But we were too afraid," another man kept repeating despairingly.

"My husband was sent away," sobbed a woman. "Then they refused to pay for me and the children to go. What are we to do now? What's going to happen to us?"

The children in the queue neither spoke nor smiled but patiently followed behind whomever they were with, staring blankly from their oddly old and wizened faces.

At last they were standing in front of the work-house master and matron. The master, a stout man with a balding head, dressed in a frock coat and striped trousers, held a list in his hand.

"Madden: Mary, Sally, and Maria," he called out.

When Emma stepped forward with the others, he frowned and turned to the matron. "I have no record of a fourth member of this family." Feeling he was about to turn her away, Emma said in as strong a voice as she could muster, "My name is Emma."

"SIR! 'My name is Emma, SIR,'" the matron screamed at her, a small stream of spittle emerging from her mouth.

"My name is Emma, sir," Emma said in a voice that was not quite steady.

"It was the relieving officer who gave orders for our admission, sir," broke in Sally. "He said we were urgent cases. Just look at me ma, sir. She's in a terrible state."

"I must have a word with that relieving officer at the next meeting of the Board of Guardians. This is not the first time he's broken rules. Doesn't he understand the importance of the paperwork when . . ."

Before the master had time to finish his sentence, he was interrupted by a woman attendant who had rushed into the room and hurried over to the Maddens. She took the woman's hand. "Oh, Mary,

I've only just heard you've been admitted." She was plainly shocked at the appearance of the woman before her.

"Ellen Flinn, you're not supposed to be in this part of the workhouse. Kindly return to your duties," the matron commanded in a high sharp voice.

"Please, sir," Ellen appealed to the master. "Oh, please. Mary Madden is a relative of mine. I think she's dying. Can't we get her to a bed right away?"

"Matron, will you ask Dr. Foley to come in again?" the master, who was a humane man, asked the disgruntled matron.

Shortly an elderly man came in and examined Mary, who had been helped to a chair against the wall. Feebly she kept saying, "Water."

"Jaundiced appearance, racing pulse, great thirst," the doctor said in a low voice to the master. "Relapsing fever."

"Can we all be together?" asked Sally anxiously.

The doctor looked at her kindly and shook his head. "No, she must go to the fever shed. Don't worry. She'll be looked after there. Now, I'd better take a look at you three."

After a brief examination he said to the matron, "No signs of fever. They're all right for the children's ward."

Tearfully Sally and Maria said good-bye to their mother, who hardly seemed to recognize them. At first Emma hung back, but when she saw the matron looking in her direction she joined them around the sick woman.

"Who's this?" whispered Ellen, nodding her head at Emma.

"She helped us at the gate. She's an orphan," explained Sally in an equally low voice. "We told the master she's a Madden."

As Mary, now too weak to walk alone, was helped to her feet by a male attendant and Ellen, the latter promised, "I'll come and tell you how she's doing."

"Where do we go?" asked Sally, clutching Ellen's hand.

"Down to the washhouse, down that corridor." She pointed to the door. "They'll give you clothes there."

"Just a minute," called the matron. "All valuables must be left here."

"But we've nothing," said Sally.

"That ring!" She pointed to Emma's ruby ring.

"It's not mine. Please don't take it away," begged Emma. "I don't own it."

"Stolen! I thought so. What would a pauper like you be doing with a ring like that?" She seized Emma's hand, pulled off the ring, and placed it on the table, beside a chipped enamel snuffbox, a few coins, and a couple wads of tobacco.

As she followed the others down the corridor, Emma began to panic for the first time since she stood outside the gates. "What's happening?" she thought.

"Where am I? How did I get here? This must be a dream. An awful nightmare. Let me wake up quick."

In the washhouse the strong smell of chloride of lime used for fumigation stung their eyes. The girls stood shivering on the bare floor; their patched dresses and threadbare underwear had been thrown into a large tub. The toothless old crone who seemed to be in charge gave each of them a rough gray dress, a shift, and a cap.

"Workhouse property," she cackled. "So if you want to run away, leave them behind. Or you'll get punished if you're caught."

"What kind of punishment?" asked Maria fearfully.

"Hang you up by the ankles," the old crone said with a grim chuckle. "A good flogging most likely. Now come on. I don't have all day."

"Where are we going?"

"The schoolroom. They'll larn you in there, I'll tell you."

They followed her through the back door of the admission block and walked along a path with bare bleak yards on either side that were bounded by high walls. Even in the open air Emma could smell the disinfectant in her wet hair.

Ahead of them was a three-story building, longer than the first block, with rows of small diamond-paned windows. "It looks like a prison," thought Emma, "apart from the windows." Inside it was cold and dark and the room into which they were led was filled with smoke from the turf fire at one end. Girls of all ages sat around on wooden forms. Some were curled up on the floor. A few were sewing bits of gray material.

"Three new ones for you, Miss Blake," the old crone shouted to the woman in charge.

"You older two can get down to sewing," said Miss Blake, shoving a bundle of material toward them. She looked at Maria's tear-stained face and disheveled fair hair. "You," she said gruffly, taking her hand, "you come and join the younger ones at the fire."

Sally and Emma sat down on the hard forms and pulled the material toward them. But they both found it impossible to concentrate. Until then, Sally had kept up a brave face. Now, putting her head down on the table, she began to sob silently.

"What is it?" asked Emma, putting her arm around the other girl's thin shoulders.

"It's Ma. Oh, Emma, will she ever get better? What are we to do if . . ." She broke off.

"Of course she'll get better. And Ellen will look after her. She promised. She'll probably take you to see her tonight." She tried to speak with a conviction she didn't feel; the sight of Mary Madden's wasted yellow face still haunted her. "But you're not to worry if Ellen doesn't come tonight. It's probably difficult for her to get away. It'll most likely be in the morning."

"It's just there are such awful stories. Of families

being parted and never seeing one another again. Not knowing if they are alive or dead."

"That won't happen. You've got Ellen, remember?"

"I suppose you're right." Sally's voice seemed a little more cheerful. "Now, maybe we'd better get started on this material."

How long they sat there Emma did not know, but when the supper bell rang, her head was splitting and her eyes were red rimmed from the smoky atmosphere. Sally went in search of Maria, and Miss Blake marshaled them all in an orderly line. They were marched into a hallway, along a corridor, and into a long gloomy room that seemed already crowded.

The meal—a mug of watery soup and a lump of bread—was eaten in total silence. Emma nearly threw up at the smell of the rancid soup and she pushed it away. Sally eagerly gulped it down, and when Emma indicated she didn't want her bread, Sally broke it into two and was about to hand half to Maria when an older girl snatched it. Emma was shocked, and even more so when she saw with what pathetic eagerness all the children fell upon their appalling ration of food. "As if they were starving," she thought, and she could hardly bear to look at the sunken eyes that stared from the gaunt faces around her.

After supper, the girls filed up narrow stone stairs to their dormitory, a large bare room with unplastered whitewashed walls and high-pitched rafters. The moment she entered the room, Emma gagged at

the heavy stale smell that came from the two vast uri-
nals at each end of the room. The others seemed not
to notice. They undressed into their shifts and lay on
the rows of mattresses, three or four children to each.
The mattresses, filled with straw, were rough and
crackled when the children lay on them.

As Emma lay beside Sally and Maria, huddled beneath a thin foul-smelling blanket, a feeling of terror
swept over her. She whispered to Sally, "This is a terrible place. I can't stay here."

"Don't worry." Sally seemed to have regained her
confidence. "It won't be long. We had an assisted passage to Canada but Ma was too sick and we were
turned back. Ma didn't want to go. I don't know why
because," her voice took on a bitter tone, "there's
nothing for us here. Maybe it was because she felt so
sick. When she's better, I'm sure she'll want to go."

"But what about me?"

"You must have some family. We'll find them.
They're probably quite near. Now, get some sleep.
Things will look better in the morning."

But as Emma stared into the darkness, where the
absolute stillness was broken only by the sound of
a stifled moan or a smothered cough, she felt more
frightened than she ever had been in her life.

If only she could wake up. Would this dreadful,
terrifying nightmare never end?

She closed her eyes tight and prayed, "Oh, God,
let me wake up."

Tragedy

A shaft of weak sunlight filtered through the diamond-paned windows and fell across Emma's face as she lay, eyes shut, trying to rid her mind of the nightmarish dream she had had the night before. It had been about a crowd of desperate people, starving people, and she was among them. They were waiting for admission to the workhouse. She'd tell her dad of it when he came. He always made her feel better after a bad dream. But she had forgotten. He wasn't coming today after all. She decided to ring him; he'd understand.

She lay quietly for a moment before turning on her side for a last doze. Soon the delicious smell of grilling bacon would be drifting up the stairs. But the noise she heard made her turn cold; it was a strange, unfamiliar sound, like something crackling. And as she moved, something pricked her skin. Why did she think of straw? Why was she lying on a straw mattress?

Forcing herself to remain calm, she thought back over the events of the previous day. She remembered trying to read *Jane Eyre*. She remembered being upset because Jean and Paul thought she was selfish and uncaring, and she had decided she was going to be different from then on. She remembered making a

19

pledge—to do a good deed for someone. But there was something else. What was it? Yes, it came back to her now. She had tried on Lucy's ruby ring and had twisted it on her finger.

Emma sat bolt upright in terror as the enormity of what had happened dawned on her. *It was the ruby ring.* The words on the box said the ring could make wishes come true. And its magic had worked. She had done something unselfish. Without thinking of her own safety in that surging mob, she had rushed to help Maria outside the workhouse. So it was no dream. What was happening now was real. She was in a workhouse somewhere in Ireland, back over a hundred years ago.

As her mind raced frantically, trying to recall what had happened yesterday, something else jogged her memory. Something about two wishes. She lay back, comforted for a moment. Now all she had to do was wish herself home again. Except that she didn't have the ring. That hateful matron had taken it from her. She'd have to get it back.

Urgently she shook Sally by the shoulder. "Wake up, I need to talk to you."

Sally sat up, worry etched on her face as she groggily rubbed her dark-circled eyes. "What is it? Is it Ma?"

"No, nothing like that," Emma assured her. "It's about my ring. The ruby ring. It doesn't belong to me. But I can't go back without it. How can I get it back from Matron?"

"Go back where?" asked Sally, puzzled.

"Where I belong." Seeing that Sally still looked puzzled, Emma went on, "Home. I can go home just as soon as I can get the ring back. Will you help me, please? I can't stay here."

"I don't see why you're here in the first place—if you have a home to go to," said Sally crossly.

Emma was silent for a moment, wondering what Sally would say if she told her she was from another time and that the ruby ring was magic. But in that prisonlike dormitory, looking at Sally's careworn face, she knew there could be little understanding of magic in the other girl's life. So she just said, "I'm a long way from home, and it's such a complicated story. Believe me when I say I can't go home without the ring. I must get it back."

Looking at Emma's upset face, Sally did not for a moment doubt that she was telling the truth. Emma figured Sally could be thinking that the ring was stolen, that she was a servant in some big house and had run away.

"If the ring is important to you," Sally said at last, "I'll ask Ellen Flinn to help. She should be able to get it for you."

"Thank you," whispered Emma gratefully.

The room had grown brighter, and Emma could

see the huddled shapes of the sleeping children on
the rows of mattresses. Sally had dropped off to sleep
again, her dark brown hair mingling with the fairer
strands of Maria's.

But Emma was wide awake, thinking only of the
ruby ring and how soon she could be back with the
McLaughlins again.

Suddenly the loud clanging of a bell shattered the
silence, heralding the start of another day in the workhouse. Almost immediately the room was alive with
the subdued activity of about a hundred girls as they
dressed in the shabby gray workhouse uniform, the
older children automatically helping the younger ones.

Down the narrow stone stairs they filed, along
a corridor, and into a dark washroom where they

washed in cold water, drying faces and hands on a filthy towel that was passed from girl to girl. Ellen was in charge and she held a whispered conversation with Sally—Emma hoped Sally would not forget to ask about the ring. But there was no time to find out because the line of children was moving into the long dining room. Silence was the rule and no one dared to speak. The master was already there, at the head of the room. He read prayers from the black book in his hand and all stood with heads bowed until he finished.

Next came roll call, and Emma could feel a trickle of perspiration run down her back as she listened. But when the name "Emma Madden" was called she went up and, like the girl before her, held out her hands for inspection by the matron. Then she was given a tin mug and stood in line to collect her breakfast—half a mug of milk and a plate of some mushy mixture.

"What is it?" she asked the girl next to her.

"Stirabout, Indian meal."

Emma tried to take a few small spoonfuls but it made her feel sick and she was relieved when a thin hand greedily took her plate. The milk had a strange half-sour taste but she managed to get it down.

After breakfast they marched back to the room they had been in the night before. Now they were separated. Emma was told to sit at the front with the older girls. Sally asked if she could sit with Maria at the back. Miss Blake, chalk in hand, wrote figures and

words on the blackboard and occasionally asked questions that nobody answered. It was, Emma thought, a
complete waste of time. When the dinner bell rang
they filed out in rows so Emma could not join Sally.
She would have to wait until they were let out into
the yard for "air and exercise," as Matron described
it. In the meanwhile she was faced with another plate
of mush.

"Skoddy," the girl beside her whispered in a low
voice. "Turnips and oatmeal mixed together. Don't
you eat it where you come from?"

"Who's talking?" shouted a voice from the top of
the room.

Emma took a mouthful. Not great but better than
stirabout. She ate it all, surprised to find how really
hungry she was.

The yard was enclosed by high walls, with a large
pile of turf stacked along one wall. In the corner of
the outside wall was a privy and a strong stench rose
from the cesspool nearby. Emma gritted her teeth
and held out as long as she could but eventually she
could wait no longer and had to enter the dark, dank,
evil-smelling place.

She joined Sally and Maria, who was running
around clapping her hands every time she saw a butterfly and chasing after it. Sally kept looking around
her. "Ellen said she'd come out when we were in the
yard," she said. "Why doesn't she come?"

"No news is good news," reassured Emma. "Your

mother must be getting better." She wondered if
Sally had asked Ellen about the ring. She waited a
few moments, but as Sally didn't mention it, Emma
decided she would have to broach the subject. "The
ring? Did you say anything to Ellen?"

"Not yet." Sally's voice sounded irritable. "It's
more important about Ma."

"I know. I'm sorry to have to bother you."

"I'll ask Ellen when she comes—if she comes."

They trudged around in silence. When they neared
the buildings at the far end, they could hear doors
banging, rough voices calling, someone shouting an
instruction. And once they heard a scream, a woman's
scream, high and desperate. It came from the Idiot
Ward. Emma gazed longingly at the patch of blue sky
above and wished she were free again.

Another bell rang. They went back to the schoolroom. More sewing. Then to supper—the same rancid soup and stale bread. Then bed.

And still there was no sign of Ellen.

In spite of her inner turmoil, fueled by her endless
imaginings of the ruby ring—when would Ellen get
it, how would she pass it over, suppose she were
caught—Emma dozed off. Then she heard the sound
of the door opening and quickly closing. She lay listening to the sound of stealthy footsteps that drew
closer and closer until they stopped beside her mattress. Opening her eyes, she sat up. It was Ellen. She
was shaking Sally by the shoulder and whispering to

her, "Get up quickly. Your mother wants to see you. She's dying. Hurry now. I don't think she'll last the night. Emma, look after Maria. Don't tell her anything."

A drowsy Maria woke up and whispered, "Ma, I want Ma. Where's Sally going?"

"Hush, you're to stay here with me. Sally will be back soon. Just go to sleep." Emma put her arms around Maria and hugged her.

"Why can't I see Ma?"

"You will, in the morning," Emma said. Maria snuggled closer. Soon her sobs subsided and she slept.

The room had been in complete darkness for some hours before Sally returned. In broken tones she whispered to Emma, "Ma is dead. I thought she'd get better and we'd still go to Canada. But that won't happen now. Everything has changed again."

The two girls lay without further talk, Sally enduring her grief silently, Emma wanting to comfort her but not knowing how. The sound of the bell released them from their two separate worlds of grief and solitude.

"What about Maria?" Emma asked Sally as they dressed. "Who's going to tell her?"

"Leave her to me. I will. Later."

Maria didn't mention being woken up in the middle of the night and seemed happy enough. After breakfast she ran out into the yard and came back with a sprig of heather.

"Pretty," she said, offering it to Emma.

In the schoolroom Miss Blake had not yet arrived. There was a strange air of detachment about Sally.

"Your mother," began Emma. "When will the funeral be?"

"What funeral? She's already buried."

"What do you mean? You have to be there. You and Maria."

"A pauper's children? Do you think they care? Besides, she wasn't buried here. The graveyard is full. It was somewhere up the road." She turned and looked at Emma. "Do you know how they bury people from the workhouse?"

"No."

"They put the body into a coffin and bring it to a pit in the ground. Then they pull a trigger, the bottom opens, and the body falls into the grave. The coffin is then taken away—for the next burial. Sometimes they don't even use a coffin. They just bring the body to the pit on a cart."

"How do you know?" asked Emma, horrified.

"When I was with Ma last night, they were all talking about fever and death and burying. . . . Well, thank God she's dead. She can't suffer anymore."

Miss Blake came in at last and the "lessons" began. Sometime during the morning Sally must have told

Maria about their mother because when they went
into dinner the little girl's face was tearstained. Afterward, out in the yard, Sally told Emma that Ellen had
promised to come out to them.

"You will ask her about the ring?"

"I will," said Sally shortly. "Tell me, is it of any
value?"

"Yes, I believe it's quite valuable. Why?"

"I thought as much. Matron wouldn't have
pounced on it if it had been just a trinket."

There was something in her voice that made Emma
uneasy. Why did Sally want to know if it was valuable?
She would have to make sure Ellen gave the ring back
to her, not to Sally.

But when Ellen came she took Sally aside and
talked to her privately and, much as she wanted to,
Emma felt she could not intrude. When Ellen left,
Sally rejoined Emma—with news that made Emma
temporarily forget about everything else.

Escape

"You said Ellen told you something important. What is it?" asked Emma nervously.

"We're being sent to Australia." Sally's face had a blank look.

"Australia? What are we going to Australia for?"

"Seems there's a short supply of labor over there. They want men, and as many unmarried girls as they can get. Of suitable character. And, of course, healthy. You and I are healthy. Not dying of fever. No wonder they examined us so closely."

"But I can't go to Australia."

"What does it matter? Here or Australia—what's the difference? And they give you a trousseau. Six shifts, two flannel petticoats, six pairs of stockings, two pairs of shoes, and two gowns, one of which must be made of warm material. Also—I almost forgot— a prayer book and a Bible. Takes a hundred days to get there."

"You sound as if you don't mind going," said Emma in a state of alarm.

"Oh, I'm not going. You see, Maria would be left behind. She's too young. Can you imagine her here all on her own? She's . . ." Sally hesitated, "not very strong. She's delicate. She wouldn't last six months here. Well, I'm not going to let that happen. We'll have to get out of here."

"Could we?" Emma snatched at the ray of hope.

"Ellen is going to help us. Now I know you want to be off home as soon as you get the ring. But I'm going to Moylough Castle with Maria, and I need you to come along."

"Moylough Castle? Where's that? And why are you going there?"

"Never mind. Ellen will get your ring back. If you want to see it again, you'll have to come with us to Moylough. I'll give it to you there."

Emma said nothing for a moment. Sally had changed. There was a hardness about her that had not been there before. As if nobody and nothing else mattered but herself and Maria.

"Doesn't look as if I will have much choice," thought Emma wretchedly. "I'm sure she means to get the ring from Ellen so I'll have to go with her. I *have* to stay close to the ring. Maybe when we get away from the workhouse, she'll be different. After all, she's just lost her mother and this place must be a painful reminder."

For a moment she thought of her own mother's death, realizing she had still not come to terms with it.

"All right, I'll come with you," she agreed reluctantly, adding, "but do you promise to give the ring back to me when we get to Moylough Castle?"

A look of relief flitted briefly across Sally's face

and she said, "Of course, I promise. Now here's the plan. We're to go in to supper and afterward to the dormitory. Don't undress. Ellen will come in to us a little later. She'll show us how to get out, and she'll have clothes and some food for us."

Emma could hardly believe it. At last she would get out of this awful place and soon she'd be home. She wondered if Maeve was out of hospital yet. She so missed them all.

As they sewed that day, Miss Blake came up with a few words of sympathy for Sally, who looked quickly at Emma as Miss Blake went on, "You two should be glad you've been chosen. You won't have to spend the rest of your days in the workhouse."

Looking around the gloomy room, Emma wondered what would happen to the rest of the children. Some would die young, she knew. Some would survive and, with help, find life outside the workhouse. Some would spend all their lives there, like the old crone in the washroom. Tears welled up in her eyes as she thought about the hopeless future that stretched ahead of so many of them. But soon, very soon, she would be free.

By supper time Emma was too tense to eat much and it was Sally who reminded her in a whisper, "Better eat now, because we don't know when we'll eat again."

Upstairs in the dormitory, Sally, Emma, and Maria slipped under their blanket and lay rigidly on the mattress. Soon afterward they heard the door opening and closing. Emma sat up urgently but Sally pulled her down again and made her wait until the soft footsteps stopped at their side. It was Ellen!

Quietly they followed her to the door. In the corridor, noises from the men's and women's wards could be heard clearly. Voices were being raised in argument. Emma feared it would bring the master or matron to restore order and they would be discovered. Then the commotion died down and all was quiet again. They crept down the stairs after Ellen, freezing when a door opened below. But nobody emerged and they reached the ground floor safely. Ellen whispered to them, "We must hurry now, before the porter locks up for the night and gives the keys to the master. He and Matron should be in the kitchen at this time, going over the stores for tomorrow. But we must make it from the front door to the admissions block without being seen or we're lost. Quickly, let's go!"

"What about my ring?" asked Emma in a panic, determined not to leave without it.

"Here!" Ellen held it up. "Matron doesn't usually leave her drawer open. But she was called away urgently and I was able to get it."

"I'll take it," said Sally, grabbing it.

Emma was about to protest but thought better of it. This was not the place to start a quarrel. Looking back at the windows that overlooked the yard, she feared discovery at every step, but they reached their

goal safely. Telling them to wait, Ellen pushed them into a dark nook under the stairs and disappeared. She returned within minutes, clutching a small bag. Thrusting it into Sally's hands she said, "You'll find three dresses and some bread in there. That's the best I can do for you. Change as soon as you can. The clump of trees down the road would be the best place. Now wait here until I see Seamus—he's the porter—and I tell him to look the other way. He promised!"

Maria started to tremble and Sally held her closer to her. Emma's heart beat faster. What if the porter went back on his word?

But soon Ellen was back. "It's all right. He'll let you out and say nothing. Now hurry. And good luck."

She patted Sally and Maria on the shoulders and gave Emma a brief nod before leading them to the heavy door where Seamus waited. With a final, "Tell Paddy and Bridie I'll be over to see them one of these days," she flitted away.

Seamus led them through the door and to the massive entrance gate. He turned the huge black key in the gate and the noise sounded as loud as thunder in Emma's ears. Would they be stopped at the last minute? But the gate eased open slightly, the children slipped through, and without a backward glance they took to their heels and ran down the road toward a small clump of trees.

The Open Road

They were still some distance from the clump of trees when they heard a shout from behind, but they did not stop. Even when they heard the sound of galloping horses, which drew nearer and nearer, they kept going. Sally dragged Maria after her, ignoring her sobbing gasps, and they plunged into the trees. Maria fell to the ground, her thin legs so weak that they could no longer support her. Sally and Emma, too, lay for a few moments, catching their breath before they crept to the edge of the trees and peered through the branches to look for their pursuer. What they saw made them clutch each other and laugh with relief. Their imagined pursuer was a horse-drawn carriage, with the driver cracking a whip over the heads of the horses and shouting encouragement.

"We'd better not stay here though. They still may come looking for us. We'll get changed as quick as we can and get out of here," said Sally, opening the bag and pulling out the clothes.

The clothes were faded and patched, but they were clean and would not be mistaken for the workhouse uniform. Sally helped Maria to get changed and let her rest a little longer before saying, "Come on, we must be going."

Cautiously they crept from their hiding place and hurried along the dusty road. Though it was late in the day it was still warm, and Emma, overjoyed at being free again, danced along, watching the sun disappear behind the trees on one side and a crescent moon rising on the other. But her sense of exhilaration was diminished when, not very far from the workhouse, they passed people dressed in rags. They were like the people she had first seen when she arrived outside the workhouse. Some lay at the roadside, too weak to go any farther, and some lay so still Emma felt sure they were dead.

"What will happen to them?" she asked unsteadily.

"The workhouse burial cart will come around in the morning and collect the dead. And maybe they'll admit some of the living, but most of them won't live long," Sally said without emotion.

They walked on in silence, Emma's mind dwelling on Sally's abrupt manner. And as they traveled along the dusty road she grew more and more resentful of the older girl's attitude toward her. Sally had no right to make her go to Moylough Castle with her and Maria.

She thought she knew where Sally had the ring. There was a small pocket in the cloth bag, and Sally patted it every now and again as if she was checking on something. Maybe she should try to grab the bag and run. But what if she was wrong and the ring wasn't there, or if Sally should overpower her? There was a toughness about her that made Emma wary. She'd have to be careful, or she might never see her ring again. The thought of not being able to return home made her footsteps falter, and Sally called impatiently, "Come on, Emma, we must hurry. It's almost dark."

"I'm so very tired. Can't we stop soon?" begged Maria.

Sally's face softened as she looked down at the wan face of the little girl at her side and she said, "Yes, we'll look for a place now."

Emma's heart beat faster when she heard this news. She thought to herself, "This is it!" Somehow she'd try and get the bag when Sally was asleep, and she'd search the little pocket for her ring. The others could carry on to Moylough Castle without her. She couldn't see why Sally thought it was so important that she came along too.

They were passing a small stream not far from the side of the road when Sally stopped and, pointing toward a rocky mound where a few ash trees grew, said, "There, that will do us for the night. Come on." They clambered over a shallow ditch, and Emma winced as her hand came into contact with the thorny spine of a whin bush growing on the other side. Sally helped Maria across and they gratefully sank down on the warm dry grass behind the rocky mound.

"There, nobody will see us here," Sally said with satisfaction. She reached into the bag and took out a chunk of bread, which she broke into small pieces, saying, "We'll have to keep some of this for the morning."

They ate in silence and even Sally laughed when Maria said, "It tastes so much better eating it out here." They drank from the stream nearby, then lay down to sleep, huddling together for warmth, Maria in the middle.

Emma had seen Sally place the bag close to her head, and she lay quietly beside the sleeping Maria for a long time before she moved. Then she quietly eased herself away from Maria's side. The young girl moved and made a small sound, so she waited tensely until she heard her even breathing again. Then she slowly inched her way to where Sally lay. She remained motionless for a few moments until she could discern the shape of the cloth bag. Taking a deep breath she stretched out her hand toward it, but let out a sudden cry of pain when her wrist was grasped tightly by Sally.

"What is it? What's wrong?" a sleepy Maria asked.

"It's all right. Everything is all right. Go back to sleep," Sally said soothingly, still holding Emma's wrist tightly. Then she said in a tired whisper, "You were looking for the ring, I suppose."

"Yes, I want to go home. And I told you I can't go back without the ring. Anyway, I can't see why you want me to go to Moylough Castle with you. Whatever it is, it's got nothing to do with me."

"And I can't see why the ring is so important to you," said Sally sharply. "You haven't told me anything

about yourself. Where you come from. Where you got the ring. Why you can't go back without it."

"I can't tell you," said Emma miserably. "It's something you wouldn't understand."

"Well, you wouldn't understand this either. It's something I must do—and I can't do it without you."

As Emma hesitated, Sally groped in the pocket of the bag and said bitterly, "I've never gotten anything from anyone in all my life. I must have been mad to expect help from a stranger. Well, if you won't help us, you won't. Here's your ring. I suppose you want to sell it and get yourself to America. You'd just about pass for age."

Silently Emma took the ring and as she gazed into

its warm ruby depths her thoughts were in turmoil. Why was she hesitating? Why didn't she just twist the ring and leave this wretched mess behind?

Then she remembered her pledge.

"Is it really so important to you?"

"Not to me. To Maria. It may affect her whole life. Oh, Emma, won't you help me?"

Still torn by indecision, Emma gave a wry smile. She had been prepared to brave burning buildings and stormy seas, yet the first time someone asked for her help she wanted to turn her back and pretend it had nothing to do with her. She took a deep breath.

"I'll come with you. But you must tell me why."

"It's about a promise I made to Ma. The night she died. She told me to go back to the castle and find Bridie."

"Who's Bridie?"

"She is—was—a cousin of Ma's."

"And she's at the castle?"

"I hope so. We were all supposed to go to Canada together. But we were turned away and Ma said Bridie and Paddy—he's her husband—weren't going to go either. The problem is that I can't look for Bridie. That's why I want you to come with us."

"Why do you have to see Bridie?"

"I don't know. Ma was too ill to talk much. But it's important."

"Sounds like a wild-goose chase," thought Emma

as she listened to the confused litany. "Going to look for someone who might or might not be there. And who may or may not have important news. What a muddle! But I'm not going back on my promise."

She handed Sally back the ruby ring. "Here, keep it for the moment. It's probably safer with you than with me."

A smile lit up Sally's thin face. "Now we'd better try to get some sleep or we won't be able to walk tomorrow."

"Is Moylough far?"

"A fair bit, but we'll manage."

As Emma turned away, Sally reached out and caught her wrist, in a friendly gesture this time. "I'm glad you decided to come. I was so worried . . ." Her voice trailed away.

As they resumed their journey next morning, Emma drank in the sweet, heavy scent of honeysuckle that grew in the hedges and admired the clumps of stately purple foxglove that flourished along the way. Once when she kicked a clump of meadowsweet, it broke into a cloud of small, sweet-scented, downy white flowers that filled the air. But the countryside was deserted. No one worked in the fields, and large tracts of land lay uncultivated, choked with weeds. A couple of carts piled high with sacks drove past.

"Bags of grain to be sent to England," said Sally bitterly.

They walked along the rough road in silence for some time until Maria, who was lagging behind, called, "Sally, can't we stop for a rest now? And, I'm hungry."

"So am I," agreed Emma.

"All right, we'll stop for a rest," said Sally, looking around her. "What about there by the river?"

Tiredly they made their way to the riverbank and drank the sparkling water before throwing themselves on the short grass to rest. They lay motionless, their limbs aching, and as they listened to the drone of the bees and the sound of the water gently lapping over the stones in the river, the three girls drifted into an exhausted sleep.

Sally woke first, and she shook the others saying, "We must have slept for a long time. We'll have to hurry. And this is the last of the bread."

"I'm still hungry," said Maria when they had eaten.

"Me too, and my feet are aching. Let's have a quick paddle in the river. It might help," suggested Emma.

Sally, looking longingly at the river, seemed about to say no, then agreed. "Right, but we must be quick."

When they emerged from the river a little later their clothes were soaking, but they felt refreshed and took turns drying their feet with the cloth bag. Then they were on their way again, the hot sun soon drying their clothes.

They passed through a small town, where most of the shops were closed up.

"We came here once or twice in the olden days," said Sally looking around her. "That was before the famine."

"What happened to everyone?"

"Moved away to big places where the hunger wasn't so bad. Worked on the roads. Went to the workhouse if they could get in—or died of starvation if they couldn't. Emigrated, as we were to do. I don't remember the famine but Ma used to talk about it. She said this was a thriving town. On Sundays and market days, men would wear frieze coats and corduroy trousers with bright waistcoats—those who could afford them, of course, not everyone. And the women wore stuff gowns, looped up to show red flannel petticoats, and caps with gay ribbons. Even, sometimes, shoes and stockings." She glanced at the warehouses on the quays, now empty and shuttered. "But even when things were really bad, the ships still came in. For the grain."

Outside the town was a graveyard, and as they passed the children could see a few people lying inside the gate, where they had collapsed and died. The girls looked at each other and, blessing themselves, hurried on.

They were now climbing uphill and the going was tough, even though the road wound through a wood, where the chestnut and beech trees on either side formed a welcome arch of cool green foliage.

"I wish we had something to eat," Maria said wistfully when they stopped to rest a few minutes.

"What about blackberries?" asked Emma, who had seen some bushes with brambles nearby.

"No, too early for blackberries. There may be some bilberries around. I'll take a look," said Sally, getting to her feet.

She hadn't been very long gone when they heard her calling and, looking at each other hopefully, the other two ran to the edge of the wood. Emma was amazed when Sally, saying, "This is all I could find that's fit for eating, I'm afraid," handed them some leaves and a few petals.

"Can we eat these?" Emma asked doubtfully.

"Of course!" Sally laughed. "Wood sorrel. Great for the thirst. And dog rose petals."

When Emma tried a little of the wood sorrel she found the tart taste pleasant and readily took another handful, mixing it with the sweet-scented rose petals.

"Keep going until the cow calves," joked Sally.

As they paused once more before reaching the top of the hill, she called excitedly, "I've found a patch of bilberries."

They fell upon the small bushes covered with blue-black berries, and when they had finished, their mouths and fingers were stained with the juice, which they rubbed off as they went along.

Sally was now running ahead, telling them to hurry. "We're almost there!"

Emma and Maria quickened their pace and at last they reached the top of the hill and emerged into the brilliant evening sunshine to join Sally. She turned to them, eyes shining, and said, "Look, there it is! That's Moylough Castle!"

Below lay a castle, a massive rectangular building with flanking towers and turreted battlements covered in ivy, built on gently sloping ground. The three children looked at each other wordlessly before they started on the winding road down, Sally and Maria running ahead, pointing to landmarks they seemed to recognize.

Emma lagged behind. So this was Moylough Castle. Now all they had to do was find Bridie. Then she could get her ring and go home. Resolutely she resolved not even to think about it.

Behind the tall gates, set in the high demesne wall, an avenue curved away into the distance. Lime trees dotted the park.

"Not that way," Sally called as Emma paused at the gate. "We go around the corner. Hurry! We mustn't be seen."

She led them along the high wall bounding the estate until she came to an open gate set in two round stone pillars. "That's the back entrance to the castle," explained Sally. The avenue swung to the right but instead of following it, Sally turned into rough pasture at the left. Shortly they were in a plantation of tall-growing trees but she confidently led the way along a winding overgrown path, and she and Maria both laughed when Emma tripped over a snaking tendril and fell flat.

"You should look where you're going," smiled Sally.

"You're not used to woods," said Maria taking her hand. "I'll help you."

Emma couldn't help smiling at the little girl's offer, but resolved to keep her eyes on the ground from then on. The forest had begun to thin. The trees became stunted and scattered and the ground was a glowing carpet of purple heather. They were at the edge of a bog.

"Maria and I will be staying here," said Sally.

"But there's no place here." Emma looked around the bleak landscape. "Only that pile of stones."

"That's it," said Sally. "That's a scalp. The remains of a cabin. Thrown down when the people who lived here left or were evicted."

"Nobody could live there!"

"Thousands live in scalps," said Sally grimly. "At least there's a roof of sorts. We'll be all right."

"What about me?" asked Emma anxiously.

"You have to go to the castle and find out where

Bridie is. Tell her Maria and I are back and I must speak to her urgently."

"But I can't just walk into the castle and start asking questions," protested Emma.

"Go to Mrs. Burke, the cook. Tell her you were sent to Moylough by Ellen Flinn, and that your family are all dead and the workhouse wanted to send you away to Australia."

"How can you be sure she'll take me in? Does she know Ellen Flinn?"

"She knows Ellen Flinn—she owes her a favor. She'll take you in all right, but remember, you're not to say anything about us. Maria and me. You escaped from the workhouse on your own."

"And what if I don't find Bridie? Suppose she's not there. What then?"

"See if you can find out where she and Paddy are and come back and tell me. As soon as you can. I know it can't be right away. But as soon as you can. Now, you'd better get to the castle."

They returned to the back avenue and Sally said, "A little farther on you'll see the walls that enclose the castle. Then you'll come to an arch on your left. That's the entrance to the kitchen yard. The door to the kitchen is just opposite."

"Is it far?"

"Not very, but when you come to see us, use the shortcut. At the end of the orchard—that's beside the kitchen yard—there's a little wicket gate. A small path—very overgrown, so mind your step—leads to a clearing in the forest. In the center there's an oak tree. Maria and I will be hiding in it during the day. Go now. And remember what I told you."

With a hurried farewell to Emma, Sally ducked under the branches and was gone.

Moylough Castle

As Emma made her way along the rutted avenue, she caught glimpses of the castle through gaps in the trees. Soon she reached the walls and, going through the archway, found herself in a cobbled yard, with a door facing her. Lifting the latch she walked into the basement of Moylough Castle.

A long passage with a flagged stone floor stretched ahead, and on her right were rows of doors, one marked "Coal," another "Wood," and a third "Dairy." In front was a stone staircase and to the left a glass-paneled door. From behind it she could hear a woman's scolding voice. It had to be the kitchen. Emma hesitated only briefly before knocking loudly and walking into a large, very hot room.

Activity ceased the moment she entered and all eyes turned toward her. Emma went over to a rotund woman who was stirring a pot on a huge black range.

"Are you Mrs. Burke?" she asked bravely.

"I am. And just how do you know my name, girl?"

"I was told to tell you that Ellen Flinn sent me," replied Emma.

"Ellen from the workhouse?" The woman's voice became friendlier and she asked, "How is she?"

"She's fine. She told me you wouldn't turn me

away," said Emma with a catch in her voice. It wasn't hard to act as if she were afraid and desperate. She was.

"Well, I owe Ellen a turn and that's the truth of it." Mrs. Burke stood silent for a moment. Then after what seemed a very long time she said, "All right, we do need an extra pair of hands. You can stay—if you're not sick. Are you? Any coughs or fever?"

As Emma shook her head, Mrs. Burke called to a girl who had stopped chopping vegetables and was eyeing Emma with great curiosity, "Here, Nancy, take . . . what's your name?"

"Emma."

"Right, take Emma here to the washhouse and then we'll find her some clothes."

In the washhouse Emma quickly scrubbed herself and washed her hair with a strong-smelling yellow soap, thinking to herself how obsessed with cleanliness everyone seemed to be. She had wrapped herself in a rough towel by the time Nancy returned. "You're to come and see Cook when you get dressed," she said, handing Emma a blue dress with a darker blue apron, a patched shift, a white cap, and wide drawers.

When Emma got back to the kitchen, Mrs. Burke was shouting instructions at a small thin girl who was collecting saucepans. "This is Annie," Mrs. Burke said. "She'll show you what to do. Normally the housekeeper hires the staff, but poor Mrs. MacWilliams has passed on and the new housekeeper won't be here until next week, so I'll take a chance. Count yourself lucky and show willing, or she'll turn you out when she arrives. That's if Lady Muck doesn't get you first. You get your bed and food and you'll work in the scullery. Annie will show you what to do and where you'll sleep. Not afraid of ghosts, are you? You'll have to sleep down here in the basement on your own for a few nights. We'll move you upstairs soon as Lady Muck is finished messing around with the rooms. Wants more storage. Thinks she owns the place already," her voice sank to a mutter and then brisked up. "Time for a little grub. You can have a bite before you get to work."

Emma followed her to the table where Nancy and Annie were already seated. Nancy passed her a plate with two currant buns and a glass of a milky liquid. The two buns disappeared in a flash. Mrs. Burke was sympathetic. "Don't give you much to eat in the workhouse, do they?" Emma took a sip of the liquid, which had a strange tart taste that she found pleasantly refreshing.

"Buttermilk," said Mrs. Burke.

Emma looked across at her and took a deep breath. It was now or never.

"I just wanted to ask you," she said timidly. "Ellen told me to ask about her cousin Bridie. And Paddy. Are they well?"

"Paddy and Bridie? Well, poor Ellen is a bit behind with the news. They've gone away. To Canada. Yesterday. On the *Thistle*. Assisted emigration. Should be nearly out of sight of Ireland by now."

"What's assisted emigration?" asked Emma.

"Lord, where were you dragged up? It's when they give you money to go away. America if you're lucky, Canada if you're not. There's even talk of Australia now. They offer you—that's the nice way to put it—a passage on the next ship calling at the nearest port—that would be Galway in these parts. Or Westport. So you take yourself and your kith and kin and sit on the quayside until some leaky ship arrives. Watched over by guards—just in case you have a change of heart. But there's no return. Soon as they get you to the highway they knock your cabin down and take over your bit of land."

"But why?" asked Emma.

"It's to do with the Poor Law. I suppose you haven't heard of that either?" Emma shook her head. "The landlord has to pay so much for every pauper he sends to the workhouse. And that can run into thousands. But some of the landlords are so poor—no rents or very little these days—they can't pay the rate. Suppose you have a thousand tenants. Cost of sending them to the workhouse is ten pounds a head a year. For ever and ever. So someone had a bright idea. Get rid of them. Pay them to go away. Anywhere. Costs ten pounds a head. And you're rid of them—forever."

"But that's terrible," said Emma.

"Well, what would you do?"

"The Clifdens don't do it," said Nancy.

"Or didn't." Mrs. Burke gave a dark look. "They certainly wouldn't approve of what's going on now. . . . Lord bless us, look at the time! Off to the scullery with the pair of you."

Emma followed Annie into the scullery, which was just off the kitchen. Copper saucepans, pots, and earthenware dishes were stacked on the floor and on the wooden draining board. Along one side there was a huge white sink, deep and long, with large brass taps.

"Do we have to clean all these now?" asked Emma faintly as she looked around.

"No, we'll leave the tougher ones steeping until tomorrow. We'll soon have the rest shining," said

Annie with a grin. "We use that silver sand and soap on them. Here I'll show you."

"What about cups and plates and glasses? Do we have to wash those too?"

"You won't come within a mile of them. They're all washed upstairs in the butler's pantry. The likes of us are not allowed to handle good china or glass." Annie chuckled at the very idea, then added, "We don't have anything to do with the main part of the castle at all. And if you ever have to go upstairs, be sure and only use the servants' stairs. They're through the door in the corner of the passage there. And don't go through any of the green baize doors on the way up. They lead on to the different floors of the castle."

They continued to work in silence for a while. Emma exerted all her energy scrubbing the difficult stains, but her mind was elsewhere. What would Sally do now?

At last Annie paused and, wiping her roughened hands on a small cloth, said, "Come on, Emma. It must be supper time. We'll leave the rest steeping."

Four other people had joined Mrs. Burke and Nancy in the servants' hall. Annie whispered their names, "That's MacGregor the butler, Hogan the footman, Agnes the laundry maid, and Hannah the housemaid." MacGregor was tall and thin with a dour, cantankerous face; Emma disliked him on sight. He stared coldly at her.

"This is Emma," said Mrs. Burke. "She's just started in the scullery."

"I thought we weren't taking on any extra help until His Lordship gets back," MacGregor frowned.

"How do you think I'm going to keep the house in order with just Nancy and Annie and Hannah?" said Mrs. Burke witheringly. "Don't forget, with Bridie going I'm a hand short in the kitchen. I want everything to be just so when the Clifdens get back."

"There is no definite news as to when they are coming back," said MacGregor stiffly. "And I would know. Either Lady Mungo or Fowler would have mentioned it to me."

"Some people don't realize the amount of work there is in a castle like this," sniffed Hannah.

Someone passed Emma a plate with a thick slice of pie on it and two pieces of bread and dripping.

"I'll be glad when the Clifdens get back. Then maybe we can get back to normal," Mrs. Burke muttered under her breath. "Getting rid of half the staff. I wonder what Lord Clifden will have to say about that."

"It wasn't half the staff." MacGregor seemed determined to contradict Mrs. Burke as often as he could. "Only the Clerys, the Kellys, and the Maddens."

Emma pricked up her ears at the mention of the Maddens, but she said nothing.

"What about Paddy and Bridie?"

"Lady Mungo had nothing to do with Paddy going. He was sore because he wasn't made gamekeeper."

"He was promised it by Lord Clifden. Hadn't Paddy been doing the work for the last year?"

"Lord Clifden hasn't been dealing with staff matters these few years. Fowler considered Paddy wasn't up to the job."

"Be that as it may," said Mrs. Burke. "He should have done nothing until Lord Clifden came back."

"And when will that be? This year. Next year. Sometime. Never. The estate has to be kept going."

"Not much evidence of that around, is there?"

"Lady Mungo has to retrench. The estate is losing, Mr. Fowler says. And as for the Maddens, they were a worthless drain."

"Mr. MacGregor, you are sitting there telling me that if the man of the family dies, his wife and two small children should be gotten rid of? Hughie Madden was a great worker until he caught the fever, and the family is one of the most respectable I know."

"That's your opinion. I regret to say you are very ill informed on these matters. You do not understand the economic background. Let me read something that sums up the problem of estates like this in a nutshell." He took a newspaper clipping from his breast pocket, smoothed it, and read aloud: "'The potato was food; it was coin; it was capital. With it has gone the nutriment of man and beast alike. Deprived of the potato, the Irish cottar is deprived of his pig. With his pig goes the rent. Thus robbed of his rent, the Irish landlord is without resources. Nay, he is in a worse condition still—is liable for the support of those on whose payments he counted for his own subsistence. He is, thus, at once poor himself and the victim of contiguous pauperism. . . .' From the *Times*, quoted in the *Cork Examiner*." He rose to his feet, folded the clipping away, and put it back into his pocket. "I'll have my pudding in the housekeeper's room. She can bring it up," he nodded at Emma. "Seeing as she's here, she might as well do a little work."

Nancy put some suet pudding on a plate and poured custard over it. "I'll show you where the housekeeper's room is."

Emma followed her out into the passage and up some stairs. "Knock before you go in," said Nancy, giving her the plate. Emma gave a timid rap and then entered. MacGregor was sitting in an armchair before the fire, puffing away at a pipe. Emma wondered if she should curtsy, then decided not.

"Knock before you enter," ordered MacGregor, who obviously hadn't heard the timid rap. "Put it," gesturing toward the plate, "on the table."

When Emma got back to the kitchen, Mrs. Burke, Agnes, and Hannah had moved to chairs before the fire and Emma joined Nancy and Annie, who were still at the table. An animated discussion was going on by the fire.

"Interfering busybody," Mrs. Burke was saying. "I understood she was to caretake the place until the Clifdens came back. Instead of which she's taken over. Why, she even tried to stop the soup kitchen Her Ladyship set up. And would have, only Mrs. MacWilliams stood her ground and said it could only end when Her Ladyship returned. That stopped her in her tracks."

"Maybe it's necessary to cut back," ventured Agnes.

But Mrs. Burke was having none of it. "And how would you know?" she said cuttingly. "I don't believe a word Lady Mungo says." She was now in full flight. "And apart from getting rid of staff, she's cutting down on kitchen stores—remember the kind of suppers I used to dish up? Everything's too good for the staff these days. But nothing's too good for herself and that curse of a son of hers."

"You should see what she's doing upstairs," said Hannah darkly. "Moving everything all over the place. That little Pembroke table has been in the drawing room as long as I can remember. She had to have it put in her own room. And that portrait of Lady Alicia, Lord Clifden's favorite aunt. She had it removed from the dining room, said she wanted to have it restored. But I saw Percy take it up to the attics."

"Doesn't surprise me in the least what she does. There's bad blood there; she was one of the Bloody Bodkins."

"Mrs. Burke!" Agnes sounded scandalized.

"It's not a swear. It's the nickname the Bodkins have. 'Bloody.'"

"Why was that?" asked Hannah.

"Way back in time the eldest son of the family was afraid his father was going to disinherit him in favor of his stepbrother. So he murdered them all. Father, mother, children. Only the baby escaped."

"What happened to the eldest son?"

"Executed. So they're known as the Bloody Bodkins. . . . And to see MacGregor fawning over her all the time. Lady Mungo this and Lady Mungo that. Makes me sick. Lady Muck, that's what she is."

"Who's Lady Muck?" whispered Emma to Annie.

"Lady Mungo Lambert. She's the wife of Lord Clifden's only brother. He was killed in a hunting accident. She's more or less in charge of the estate at the moment. She has a dreadful son, Percy. If you meet him, run the other way."

"Do the Clifdens have any children?"

"There was one. That was a dreadful tragedy. About six months ago . . ."

"What are you three gossiping about?" called Mrs. Burke. "Clear up here and off to bed with you—or you won't be fit for the day's work I've planned for you."

"What time do we get up?"

"Six on the dot. I'll call you," said Nancy.

She led Emma along the corridor leading from the

kitchen and into a small dark room. "This is where you'll sleep. I share a room with Annie on the third floor. At least you have a room to yourself, even if it's down here."

As Emma looked around the tiny room with a narrow bed, a washstand with jug and basin, and a small barred window, she thought, "At least there's a mattress." She remembered the hardness of the ground the night before. "And it's a whole lot better than the workhouse." She wondered if this was how Jane Eyre felt when the cruel regime at Lowood was replaced by a more humane one.

"Am I the only person sleeping down here?"

Nancy giggled. "Usually the men servants sleep down here, the women upstairs. But MacGregor has a place of his own and Hogan now sleeps in the stable block. Poor Eddie. He's terrified of horses but Fowler—he's the estate manager and looks after the horses and stables—sacked the two stable boys and told Eddie that as he had very little to do with the Clifdens away, he'd have to give a hand with the mucking out."

As Emma stretched her tired limbs she thought of the events of the day and wondered how Sally and Maria were getting on at the scalp. She would try to visit them as soon as possible the next day, though it would hardly be before the six o'clock start. She would have to bring them something to eat—and how on earth was she to manage that? She resolved to slip half of anything she got to eat into her apron pocket.

As she lay there, she stored up in her mind all she had learned so far so that she could relate it to Sally. Paddy and Bridie had gone to Canada; it was their decision, according to MacGregor.

Lady Mungo had taken charge of the castle while the Clifdens had been away. No one liked her or her son and it was she, aided and abetted by Fowler, who seemed to be an important person, who had arranged for the Madden family to emigrate.

"But why?" she wondered, puzzled. The Clifdens were rich, according to Mrs. Burke. They didn't have to get rid of tenants to save money. Or did they? MacGregor said the estate was losing money. A widow and two small children were a liability.

She was still trying to work it out when, exhausted, she fell asleep.

The Oak Tree

Emma awoke before sunrise and lay for a moment, heart beating anxiously, thinking she was still in the workhouse. Then she remembered with relief that she was at Moylough Castle. She wondered what time it was. Everything was so quiet. Should she risk going to the kitchen to search for some food to take to Sally and Maria? She hoped they weren't too hungry at this stage and, knowing Sally, Emma was sure she would have kept back some of the bread as a reserve.

Jumping out of bed, she slipped on her dress, and in her bare feet padded softly along the corridor to the kitchen door. Opening it quietly, she peeped inside and saw that the room was empty. A quick look at the wall clock showed that the hands pointed at twenty to six. The dresser was huge and the racks above her head were stacked with plates, while patterned cups hung from rows of hooks. Copper saucepans of all sizes were placed around the walls. On the shelf of the dresser were four large crockery bins. Gingerly removing the lid of the first one, she saw it was almost full of bread. The second one was filled with buns. With a nervous look over her shoulder, she grabbed four buns and gently replaced the lid. She took a muslin cloth and, wrapping the buns in it, put them in her deep pocket. Within a matter of minutes, she was back in her room.

Shortly after, a light tap on the door brought Nancy, who said, "Good, you're up. I need your help in the kitchen."

Emma pulled on her boots and splashed cold water from the jug on her face and hands. She tidied her hair with the wide-toothed comb provided, tucked her hair under her cap, and followed Nancy into the kitchen. She was instructed to carry two pails of ashes through the scullery and out into the yard.

"O'Flaherty—he's the odd-jobs man—will deal with them later," said Nancy, adding, "then you can fill the boiler with water."

Annie had already started work and smiled at Emma. "Well, Emma, how did you sleep on your first night?"

"Fine," Emma smiled back, thinking it was paradise compared to the workhouse, even if the mattress was just a series of lumps.

The fire was blazing in the range when she got back and she could hear the water already singing in the heavy black kettle when she went to fill the boiler.

"No, not that one," shouted Nancy as she lifted the lid. "That's the stockpot. Cook or myself will see to that one. The long one is the boiler. You'll soon learn."

"Indeed she will!" agreed Mrs. Burke, who had

just come into the kitchen, adding, "After breakfast you can help Annie get the vegetables ready. It's carrots and turnips today."

Breakfast was a large plate of porridge and two thick slices of bread. Afterward Emma helped Annie to peel buckets of turnips and scrape loads of carrots.

"Such a huge amount," she said, somewhat bewildered. "Surely we won't eat all this."

"We won't," explained Annie. "Most will be used for soup for the paupers. That's made in a huge pot in the kitchen yard. Usually by O'Flaherty." Seeing that Emma looked astonished, she laughed. "Anyone could make it. It's just water and vegetables, sometimes a bit of bacon."

"And when do the. . . ," she hated using the word, ". . . paupers get it?"

"They stand around all morning waiting, usually it's ready about eleven or twelve—there now, I think we've finished. We're taking the vegetables to the yard now," she called as they passed through the kitchen.

"All right and don't be all day about it. Get right back here. I want all the jelly molds cleaned today."

"Is it always as busy as this?" Emma asked as they crossed the yard outside the kitchen.

"Wait until the family gets back. Things will really get busy then."

"How many are in the family?"

"Only Lord and Lady Clifden. But it's not just the two of them. There's Lady Clifden's maid and Lord

Clifden's valet. Then they'll probably have guests to stay and they'll all bring personal servants. We'll be worked off our feet," she finished cheerfully.

They crossed the cobbled kitchen yard and went through a wide arch into another yard. In the center was a blazing fire and, sitting on top, the biggest pot Emma had ever seen. It was of cast iron and stirring it was a thin wizened man with a stoop. "This is O'Flaherty," whispered Annie. "Don't let him keep you here talking. Once he starts, he never stops."

"What kept you?" He grinned at Annie. "You're getting lazy on me. Who have we here?"

"This is Emma."

"Emma who?"

"Martin," supplied Emma.

"Martin! Well, well, well . . . I could tell you . . ."

Just then a massive black horse trotted into the yard. Its rider, a thickset man, jumped off and tossed the reins to O'Flaherty.

"That's Fowler, the estate manager," whispered Annie. "Come on, quick."

She pulled Emma after her through another arch at the top of the yard. "Let's go into the orchard, get ourselves some apples."

The fruit was just beginning to ripen and Annie picked two apples. She tossed one over to Emma, then sat down on a bank and began to eat hers. In spite of Mrs. Burke's injunction, she seemed in no hurry to get back.

"What's in there?" asked Emma, pointing to an ornate gate, with stone pillars on each side, topped by carved stone pineapples.

"The gardens. There are steps down from the castle to the lawns. The walled garden for fruit and vegetables is on the other side. There's a beautiful walk along the back. Ladies' Walk. Very secluded. Cook says it's for courting couples."

"I'll just take a look around."

"Well, don't go far. And don't go into the gardens. They're strictly out-of-bounds."

"I won't," said Emma, racing off. A daring plan had formed in her mind. She would go and see Sally and Maria! It need only take a few minutes.

At the back of the orchard she found the little wicket gate Sally had told her about. Birds flew from the trees as she ran beneath them and once she was startled by the flash of a bushy tail as a red squirrel ran up a tree just in front of her. Then she was in the clearing and there were Sally and Maria, sitting at the base of the oak tree.

"We thought you were never coming," said Sally getting up.

"Sorry, I couldn't get here any sooner. It was impossible. As it is, I've just about two minutes or Annie will be after me. Not to mention Mrs. Burke."

"What about Bridie? Did you find her?" asked Sally urgently.

"No, I didn't and . . ." She hardly knew how to say it. Then it came out in a burst. "She's gone. With Paddy. To Canada."

"Canada!" Sally looked dismayed. "But they weren't to go. Ma said they weren't going to go. Unless—maybe they came back here, were found, and sent off again. Oh, Emma, what do we do now? I have to find Bridie."

"I'll see what I can do. The trouble is I don't want to ask Mrs. Burke too many questions. Is there anyone else?"

"There's an old man in the kitchen yard. O'Flaherty," said Sally slowly. "He's been there for centuries. Ma used to say he knew everything that was going on."

"I've met him just now. I'll ask him as soon as I can."

"Did you bring anything to eat?" Maria, who had been dancing around, came rushing back to them.

"I almost forgot," said Emma, producing the buns and the apple. "I'll get you more tonight. Where will I meet you? Here?"

Sally nodded. She put her foot on a large burr at the side of the oak tree under which they had been sitting and, grasping an overhanging branch, pulled herself up—and disappeared.

"There's a hollow here," she called down. "It's our hiding place." She dropped to the ground again. "But make sure nobody sees you. And don't speak. Make a call like this." She put her hands to her mouth and made a soft cooing noise, "Oo-oo-ooh."

Emma tried but the sound she produced was so harsh that Sally burst out laughing. "Nobody would ever mistake you for a long-eared owl. Try this." She made another sound, "Coor-cooo, coor-cooo. That's a wood pigeon."

Emma tried again and though Sally and Maria hid their smiles at her effort, it was agreed that it was a passable imitation.

Lady Mungo

When Emma got back to the bank where she had left Annie eating her apple, Annie had gone. Emma gave a groan. She would be late back from the soup run and who knew what Mrs. Burke might do. Sack her? In panic she ran as hard as she could to the kitchen.

Just as she neared the arched entrance, a tall heavily built youth leaped out of the bushes and caught her by the arm.

"Who have we got here?" he shouted, pulling at her hair until it escaped from the cap she was wearing. "Haven't seen you before, have I? What's your name, girl?"

"Let me go," said Emma angrily. Twisting herself from his grasp she gave him a violent shove and, losing his balance, he fell backward into the bushes. Before he could get up, she was through the arch, across the yard, and into the kitchen.

To her surprise, a number of people were gathered there. Mrs. Burke, Agnes, Hannah, Nancy, and Annie, standing in a group, were being addressed by a tall, severe-looking woman with thin pursed lips. She was standing straight as a ramrod, her hands clasped before her. Behind her was MacGregor. As she turned slightly to focus on Emma, her dark dress, trimmed with rich-looking lace, gave a silken rustle.

"Oh, no," Emma groaned to herself as she hurriedly tried to push her hair up beneath her cap. "Lady Muck!"

"And who is this . . . creature?" asked Lady Mungo. "And what is she doing here?"

There was a further disturbance as the youth dashed in and rushed up to Lady Mungo. "She hit me, she hit me."

"Who hit you?"

"She did," pointing to Emma.

"He grabbed me," said Emma defensively. "I was trying to get away."

"How dare you speak!" rasped Lady Mungo.

"This is Emma," put in Mrs. Burke. "She's the new scullery maid."

"Why wasn't I told about this?"

"Mrs. MacWilliams, God rest her soul, agreed we could get someone extra. I understand His Lordship and Her Ladyship may be coming back soon."

"Their return is not altogether certain," said Lady Mungo, pursing her lips even more. "I haven't had confirmation yet. As for this girl, remember in the future that all staff matters must be referred to me." Then she turned to the youth. "Percy, go upstairs. I've told you before, you're not to come into this part of the castle, the servants' quarters."

As Percy passed by Emma, he hissed at her, "Just you wait. You'll pay for this yet."

When he left, Lady Mungo resumed her address to the staff.

"As I was saying, this is a very serious matter. A valuable painting has disappeared from the dining room. Someone has taken it. I want it back at once."

"It's the portrait of Lady Alicia, Lord Clifden's aunt," supplied MacGregor.

"Are you suggesting someone has stolen it?" Mrs. Burke asked indignantly. "That's absurd."

"Well, it has disappeared and can't be found."

"Maybe someone put it up in the attics," said Mrs. Burke guilelessly. "For cleaning or something."

"Well it's not there now," frowned Lady Mungo.

"It could have been." MacGregor coughed and bowed slightly to Lady Mungo. "One or two old servants occasionally come to spend a night in the attics. It's by permission of Lord Clifden. They would come in through the kitchen and go upstairs by the servants' stairs. Usually they're harmless, but the painting may have been a temptation."

"A most improper arrangement," said Lady Mungo. "I direct you to question them about the painting." And as Mrs. Burke raised her eyes to heaven, Lady Mungo swept from the kitchen, followed by MacGregor.

It was now one o'clock and the stew that had been ready and merrily simmering away on the range since twelve noon was ladled out.

"Doesn't that beat Banagher?" declared Mrs. Burke. "Hiding the picture away in the attics, then announcing it's been stolen from the dining room. Accusing one of us of stealing it."

"She didn't exactly," said Agnes. "She said it was missing."

"Well, my money is on Percy. Who else would take a painting? Where would they sell it? The woman is mad. And as for MacGregor and his 'old servants,' the only people who sometimes spend a night or two in the attics are Liza and Finnegan the lamp man. I can't see either of them making off with a famous portrait and pretending it came from their scalps up the mountains. It's my belief she intended it to disappear. Then it *did*. Now she's heard the rumor that Lord Clifden is coming back and it's panic stations."

"No wonder she's so upset about it," said Agnes. "He'll blame her."

"He won't," said Mrs. Burke shortly. "Hannah may have seen Percy taking it upstairs, but who's going to take her word? Lady Muck will blame someone else. Well, I won't stand for it."

Afterward, as Annie and Emma cleaned the jelly molds in the scullery, Emma asked, "Why all the fuss about the painting. Is it very valuable?"

"It's a portrait of Lord Clifden's aunt, Lady Alicia, his father's sister, painted when she was very young. I've never seen it myself, but they say she was very pretty. Lord Clifden was devoted to her."

"What do you think happened to it?" asked Emma.

"I think Lady Muck stole it," giggled Annie. "I

think she intended to sell it. She's not all that well off, I believe."

"Surely she couldn't do that. Wouldn't she be found out? Then what would the Clifdens say? Is it true that they're coming back soon?"

"Mrs. Burke thinks so—and she may well know. One of the servants they brought with them, a young fellow called Jamie, is her nephew."

"Why have they been away for so long?"

"It was on account of Lady Charlotte."

"Is that the child you started to tell me about last night before we were sent to bed?" asked Emma.

"Yes. It's a very sad story. I wasn't here when she was born but I was here when she died—that was about six months ago. She hadn't been well for some time. I remember they used to bring her into the garden when the weather was fine and put her sitting in a chair, propped up with cushions. I used to wave to her when I was in the orchard, and she would wave back. Poor thing, she must have been very lonely, all by herself. I hadn't seen her since last autumn because, naturally, she wasn't out in the winter. Then she took the fever and they couldn't do nothing for her, even though they had doctors from Dublin, even from London. She was only seven and so pretty. Long dark hair. It broke both their hearts. That was why they went away. To Italy they say. People said they would never return."

"I wonder what will happen about the painting?"

"It'll turn up of course and be put back in the dining room. And one of us will be blamed for taking it."

"Probably me," thought Emma, remembering the icy glance Lady Mungo had thrown her when she was leaving the kitchen.

"There, that's the last of the jelly molds," said Annie, holding one up. "Don't they polish up well? Now back to the kitchen to see what Mrs. B. has cooked up for us for the rest of the afternoon."

But whatever plans Mrs. Burke had, they had been changed. With a face like thunder she told them they were to spend the next few hours searching the attics. Orders from Lady Mungo!

"That painting. She says it must be found. What are we to do if it *has* disappeared? Will anybody tell me that? Pity we can't look in Master Percy's room. It'll be a wasted afternoon and we won't get a stroke of work done."

Emma was rather delighted they didn't have to spend the afternoon scouring and polishing and scrubbing, even though she knew the work would have to be done tomorrow. It was a reprieve for the moment.

The attics looked as if they hadn't been touched for years. Old pieces of furniture, rolled-up carpets, boxes of cracked china, trunks full of old clothes were stacked in every room.

"If you put anything down in any of these rooms, you'd never find it again," laughed Nancy. "How do you fancy this?" She had delved into one of the trunks in the first room, picked out a hat with a huge feather plume, and paraded around, tossing her head this way and that.

"Let's dress up," suggested Annie, taking out a dress with mangy fur braiding around the collar, cuffs, and hem.

"Let's do nothing of the sort," snapped Mrs. Burke, who had just appeared, breathless from the steep and winding circuit of the servants' stairs to the top floor. "Come on, we've no time to waste. Nancy, you search this room thoroughly. Look behind everything. The painting may have been pushed under something. Annie, you take the next room, and Emma the one on the other side. I'll do the end room. Then we'll search the other side of the corridor."

They split up and Emma began a detailed search of the room she was allotted. Less crowded than the rooms Nancy and Annie had been assigned to, it seemed to have been a bedroom of some kind as there was a bed in one corner with disturbed clothing, as if someone had just left it. Maybe someone had been sleeping there and had hastily left on hearing the advance of the search party. But of the painting there was neither hide nor hair.

Emma went back into the corridor, but the other three were still searching their rooms. A heavy red plush curtain hung about halfway down, looped up at one side. Emma peered through the opening and saw more doors. At this rate it would take them until

sunset to get through the rooms! Then, suddenly, a
figure came out of the farthest door. It was an old
woman and her back was to Emma. At this moment
Emma sneezed. The figure turned quickly, then glided
away again.

"I wonder, would she know anything about Paddy
and Bridie?" thought Emma. "If she comes from the
village and was down there this morning, maybe she
has some news of them. She might know if their ship
sailed, or if it maybe was delayed. At least I'd have
something to tell Sally."

She dashed after the old woman—then drew back
in surprise. She was nowhere to be seen! She must
have gone into that end room, thought Emma. But

there was no sign of her there. The only hiding place was an ancient-looking chest against the wall, but the door refused to open. It seemed to be locked. The old woman had simply disappeared into thin air. Emma went out again to the corridor. A few yards from the door a small window looked over the walled garden. There was no staircase to the lower floors at this end. Quickly she looked into the other rooms beyond the curtain. Nothing. Just more junk. Yet the old woman had vanished. Where had she gone?

"Emma," a sharp voice called, "where are you?"

"I finished my room," replied Emma. "I was just looking in the one down here."

The attic search took another hour. Then Mrs. Burke sent Hannah down to tell Lady Mungo that the painting was definitely not in the attics.

Emma sneezed again on the way down to the kitchen and Mrs. Burke looked at her with concern. "I hope you're not taking ill?"

"It's just the dust," said Emma, sneezing again.

"Typical! Just when I need everyone in the full of their health. Take a walk, girl. Get some air into those lungs. Don't want anyone sneezing about the place when the family come back. Here," Mrs. Burke delved into her pocket and pulled out a piece of paper and pencil, "take this to O'Flaherty. It's about tomorrow's soup. If anyone asks you what you're doing in the orchard, say I sent you to see him."

Emma could hardly conceal her delight. Now she

had an excuse to see him. She flew down the stairs, ahead of Nancy and Annie, and darted through the door into the yard. A voice called to her from one of the stone buildings and O'Flaherty came out.

"I have a note for you," she said, thrusting it into his hand. "About the soup. From Mrs. Burke."

"And how is she? A great friend of mine, Mrs. Burke." He read the note and glanced at Emma.

"Tell Mrs. Burke it's true. I had word from Jamie. The Clifdens are on the way. Tomorrow or the next day . . . and I've another bit of news for her."

"What?" asked Emma. Sally said he knew everything that went on. But he seemed in no hurry to impart his bit of news to her.

"Emma Martin." He lingered on the word "Martin." "Strange, isn't it, that we're both standing here. O'Flaherty and Martin. On the same side."

"What's strange about that?" said Emma, wishing he'd get around to giving her the news.

"Wasn't like that in the old days. You see the Martins were one of the tribes—Normans—and the O'Flahertys were the wild Irish."

"Yes, I know. 'From the fury of the O'Flahertys, good God deliver us.'"

"Now, that's good. They still remember. Only thing the O'Flahertys and Martins had in common—and a poor thing it was—was the Stuarts. We were all toppled by Cromwell." There was a pause. "Now, if someone took everything you had, what would you do?"

"I don't know." Emma tried not to sound impatient.

"You'd turn and grab someone else's property. That's what the Martins did to us. Quarter of a million acres, in Connemara. The 'wild territories.' This castle too. Did you know it was once an O'Flaherty castle?"

"Mr. O'Flahrety, you said you had some news. What is it?"

"It's about Paddy and Bridie."

"We know," said Emma, disappointed. "They've left. On the . . ." She couldn't remember the name of the ship. "They left yesterday."

"Did they now?"

"What do you mean?"

"Now, for your ears only—and Mrs. Burke's, of course—it's said they didn't go. They were missing when they rounded up the batch."

As the full significance of his words sank into Emma's brain, her face lit up. Paddy and Bridie were still in Ireland! Sally would be pleased. Bridie could give her whatever information she wanted and she, Emma, would be on her way home again. Maybe by this time tomorrow she would be back in her own time and with her own family. She would see her dad and Helen again. And Maeve. She had tried not to think of them. Now she could!

Then her face clouded over. If Paddy and Bridie hadn't taken the boat—and O'Flaherty's words were

"It's said"—where were they? They could be any-where. Gone to distant relations possibly. In that case, Sally must know where they were.

"Thanks, Mr. O'Flaherty," she said before turn-ing and dashing out into the orchard along the path she had taken that morning.

The Priest's Hole

When she reached the clearing, Emma gave the soft
"Coor-cooo, coor-cooo" call. Two seconds later Sally
and Maria appeared, and Emma gave them the bread
she had taken from the kitchen and some pieces of pie.

"There's news of Bridie and Paddy," she said
breathlessly. "They may not have taken the boat.
O'Flaherty says he thinks they didn't. So they must
be somewhere around. You should know, Sally."

"Bridie was from Carnmore, about twenty miles
from here. That's a long way off," said Sally despond-
ently. "They've both probably gone to her relatives.
How are we going to get in touch with them? Emma,
you'll have to go back to O'Flaherty. He may have
news of where they are."

Emma's heart sank. So she wouldn't be home this
time tomorrow. She sat down beside Sally and said
softly, "Sally, why is it so important for you to see
Bridie? You must tell me. Maybe if I knew, I could
be of more help."

"It was the night Ma died," said Sally sadly. "She
was so weak she could hardly talk. When I went in to
see her she caught me by the hand. Her hands, they
were so thin and wasted. She dug them into my arms
and clung to me. And all she kept saying was, 'You

must see Bridie. Bridie knows something of great importance.'

"I said, 'How can I see Bridie? She and Paddy have gone to Canada.'

"She replied, in a very low voice so nobody would hear, that they hadn't. That I was to go to Moylough and find them. But that neither Maria nor I were to go near the castle. I couldn't get anything else out of her. She wasn't listening to me. She just kept saying, 'You have to see Bridie. It's very important for Maria. Will you promise me?' Over and over again. Of course I promised, but I don't think she even heard me. Her mind wandered and she thought she was back in Bridie's old home again. Then Ellen came and took me away. Later she told me Ma was dead."

"How did you know Bridie?"

"She was always there, as long as I can remember. She was some kind of cousin of Ma's and they lived together when they were children, though Ma was older—Ma's father and mother had died when she was very young and Bridie's family took her in. When she was about fourteen, Ma came here—to Moylough— to work. Later when she married Da she stopped being full time. She had always kept in touch with Bridie, so Bridie got Ma's old job. That's how Bridie met Paddy, who worked here too."

"What happened to your father?"

"He's dead. It happened this spring. About the time Lady Charlotte died. It was the same fever. A lot of people around here died of it. With Da gone, it was desperate, even though Lord Clifden ordered that Ma need pay no rent for the time being. We didn't starve, but it was tough. Ma used to help out in the kitchen, and she got odd work at the farmhouses. Bridie was great. She brought us food, and she used to say that when Paddy was made gamekeeper we could all go to live with them. We were looking forward to that." Her eyes clouded over and she turned away for a moment.

"Go on," whispered Emma.

"Everything changed when Lady Charlotte died. The Clifdens were in a daze. And suddenly, within a week, they were gone. Lady Mungo had come to Moylough when Charlotte was ill; she was as sweet as honey. The Clifdens were completely taken in by her. Even before they went away she was running things. Then when the Clifdens left she was in complete charge of the estate. She started putting her own people in, like MacGregor. She didn't want Ma and lots of other people who used to work here, and she stood in the way of Paddy getting to be gamekeeper. She and Fowler decided everything. I still got food at the castle, but once when I went to the kitchen door to collect it, she ordered Nancy to shut the door in my face, said she was tired of having paupers all round her.

"Then a few days ago Fowler came by. Ma wasn't there so he gave me the message, sitting on that great black horse of his, talking down to me. We were to be evicted on Lady Mungo's order, and the cabin was to be knocked down. She couldn't turn us out on the roads because she was afraid Lord Clifden might find out, so we were to be sent away. Our passage to Canada was to be paid.

"I didn't care at that stage. With Da dead and things the way they were, I felt anything was better than staying in Ireland. Especially as Paddy and Bridie had been ordered to go too. But Ma went mad. Said she would never leave the estate. They had to drag her out of the cabin before they knocked it down."

"And then?"

"We were on our way to Galway when Ma got sick. Her mind was wandering, she didn't know where she was. Anyway, the end of it all was that they wouldn't take us—we were sent to the workhouse. That's when you came along."

Emma got to her feet. She hated leaving Sally but knew that Mrs. Burke must be waiting for the message from O'Flaherty. But before she left, she had one last question for Sally. "Why was Bridie so important? How could she have helped you?"

"I don't know," answered Sally. "I'm tired of wondering about that. Unless. . . . Bridie's sister worked for a farmer's wife not too far from here. She, they, had no children. She came over to see us a few times and was very taken with Maria. Maybe she wanted to take her to live with them."

"But then you would be all on your own."

"Yes, but I wouldn't mind if it gave Maria a better chance in life. Imagine—a farm. Proper food and no lack of it. Clothes. I love Maria. She deserves better than having to live in a scalp."

"And so do you," thought Emma. "You're the most unselfish person I know." But she didn't say anything, just pressed Sally's hand.

As she turned away, she had a sudden thought. To cheer Sally up, she told her about the woman who had vanished in the attics.

"I told Annie about it," she said laughing. "She told me that if it had been a young girl it might have been Lady Charlotte come to haunt us, but ghosts don't come out until night."

"Vanished? What do you mean?"

"I was looking down the corridor, and I definitely saw an old woman—she was short and fat—standing there. I started toward her. Then she disappeared into thin air."

"Where exactly?" asked Sally in great excitement.

"The corridor in the attics. You come up the stairs, and there's this corridor, with a window at the other end. I think she went into the last room."

"That's it!" exclaimed Sally. "The priest's hole! Ma told me about it. There's a secret closet opening off that room. You press the wall in a certain place and it slides open a little bit. Just enough to let someone squeeze through." She gave a little jump and

clapped her hands. "How stupid I've been. That's where Paddy and Bridie are hiding out! Emma, I think I'm beginning to piece it all together. Ma was definite Paddy and Bridie weren't going to Canada. That I was to come back here to Moylough and find Bridie. Ma must have known she would be here. But she'd forgotten they would have had to hide."

"Why? Couldn't they have gone back to their old cabin?"

"No. It would have been reported that they didn't turn up at the quayside—so a search would have been made for them, to put them on the next ship. That's why they had to hide."

"Wait a minute," said Emma. "They wouldn't hide

in the castle, right under the noses of Lady Mungo and Fowler. Wouldn't that be the first place anyone would look?"

"Hardly anyone knows about the priest's hole. It was put in ages ago when priests were forbidden to say mass. They would escape through the hole if any soldiers came around. There's a very small window there looking over the entrance courtyard. That way they could look out and see the soldiers arriving and departing. Ma said it was also used by rebels in 1798."

"And you're sure nobody knows about it?"

"Quite sure. It's part of the very old castle. The people who built it were dispossessed by Cromwell, who gave it to a friend of his. Later the Clifdens bought it, about fifty or sixty years ago. The older servants here would know about the priest's hole. Da's family too, they come from here. That's how Ma knew about it, and she told me. I was sworn to secrecy. Not even Maria knows."

"Have you ever been there?"

"No, that's why I don't know exactly how you get into it. Emma, you've got to go up there, find it, and talk to Bridie."

"But how? We're not allowed upstairs."

"But you went up today."

"That was special. We were all sent up to the attics to look for a missing painting."

"You must think of something else and get up. Emma, you'll have to help us. It's our only chance."

"I'll try," said Emma dubiously.

Going back through the woods, she thought it a tall order. Even if she managed to slip away and get back up to the attics, how would she find the priest's hole? The directions were hopelessly vague. And in spite of what Sally had said, she didn't really believe Paddy and Bridie could be hiding in the castle. And when Lady Mungo found out they hadn't gone to Canada, she would order a search for them. Fowler would be in on the hunt.

Emma shivered to herself as she wondered what would happen next.

"And about time too," grumbled Mrs. Burke when Emma got back to the kitchen. "I didn't mean you to stay out all evening. Did you see O'Flaherty?"

"Yes, he asked me to tell you Paddy and Bridie didn't go away—and the Clifdens are coming back. Tomorrow. Or the day after."

A smile spread over Mrs. Burke's face, florid from stooping over a hot range and a delicious-smelling stew. "Well, that's one for Lady Muck!"

Supper that night was a cheerful affair. And the fact that MacGregor didn't appear but had his supper sent up to the housekeeper's room heightened the air of gaiety.

Mrs. Burke was in a reminiscent mood. "The poor Clifdens. But no matter what, they're better off here at home instead of some foreign place. They'll have to accept poor Lady Charlotte is gone. How well I remember the day she was born. Lady Clifden was so ill we all thought she'd die. Then Lady Alicia—Lord Clifden's sister—came. She was the godmother—dead now, poor soul. And all that seemed to bother her was that little Charlotte didn't have the Clifden birthmark. All the heirs have it."

"But Charlotte wasn't necessarily the heir," said Agnes. "The Clifdens might have had a son."

"If they didn't, Lady Charlotte would inherit," said Mrs. Burke firmly. "The titles can descend through the female line. When the Lamberts voted for the Union . . ."

Emma listened, yawning. "Why are they all so interested in history and things that happened ages ago?" she thought. She shut her ears to the talk and tried to figure out how she could get back up to the attics.

Ladies' Walk

The news that the Clifdens were definitely on their way home had a galvanizing effect on Mrs. Burke. In high good humor, she ordered a complete clean up. Cupboards were opened and tidied, passages swept out, shelves washed down again, and Hogan called in to clear out the coal and wood houses. Even the yard was spruced up. After a hectic morning washing and scrubbing and polishing until everything in the kitchen, pantries, and the whole downstairs area sparkled or shone, Mrs. Burke called a halt and they all sat round the kitchen table.

"Just like the old days," she said, looking around her with pride. "I remember Lady Clifden and poor little Charlotte coming in to see us, and Lady Clifden would always say how splendid the place looked, with the wooden tables scrubbed until they were like snow, the kitchen tiles looking like they were polished, and the fire glowing away in the range. All we can hope for now is that another little one is on the way, and Lady Muck and Percy are sent packing." She paused for a moment. "What are we going to give them? Nancy, fetch down my recipe book."

Nancy went to the dresser and took down a big black book, which she handed to Mrs. Burke, retrieving several loose bits of paper that had fallen out. Mrs. Burke picked them up. "Charlotte russe— lord no! . . . Crimped salmon—we're a bit late for that. . . . Nesselrode pudding—no chestnuts. . . . Dear me, is there anything in season this time of year? Let's see," she said, flicking the pages of the black book. "Asparagus soup—Nancy, check the kitchen garden. Turbot—Annie, get O'Flaherty to send a message to the fish people in Inishbeg. Roast haunch of venison— where's Paddy when we need him? Still it's a lot of bother with all those hot-water plates."

"Hot-water plates?" queried Emma.

"There's a dish beneath filled with hot water. To keep the fat from getting cold. Tastes awful if it does. Roast grouse—well, I can't go out and shoot them, and Fowler's gem of a gamekeeper hasn't turned up yet. It'll have to be mutton—rolled loin of mutton—at least we have that on hand. Good, well-flavored mutton, much better than lamb. No flavor, I always say. With port, mushrooms, and red currant jelly. Then for afters: jelly molded with fresh fruit—*Macédoine de Fruits,* they call it—and Her Ladyship always loves my greengage tart. Apple crumble for Lord Clifden—he was so fond of my apple crumble, especially this time of year. 'First of the season,' he'd say. Emma, run along to the orchard and pick me some of those White Transparent—they're the first ones to ripen. I'll make a pie and some crumble."

Delighted, Emma got up, wondering if she could take some food with her. But because Mrs. Burke was sitting facing the dresser, she had to pass by the bread bins. Luckily the cold storage pantry for meat was out of the servants' line of vision, so she took a few slices of cold mutton.

It was a soft mild day, autumn already in the air, the sun warm but not hot, crisp leaves underfoot, dew still lying in sheltered grassy nooks. But Emma had other things on her mind. How was she going to get upstairs and search for the priest's hole? Maybe she would get a chance after dinner, when Mrs. Burke always went for a nap. But that meant she would have to get by the bedrooms on the third floor to get to the door that led to the attics. Maybe it would be better to try now, when the servants were in the kitchen or out on messages.

When she had gathered the apples, she couldn't resist the temptation to have a peep into the garden. But it was a disappointment. The rose bushes were straggly and unkempt, the weeds rampant in flower-beds and on paths. She went down toward Ladies' Walk, but it too was neglected and overgrown.

She was just about to return to the orchard when she saw figures come out onto the terrace of the castle. They were coming down the steps and would soon be walking toward her along the center path of the garden. Emma froze. She couldn't cross the lawn to get back into the orchard without being seen. She would have to hide. She squeezed through the thick shrubbery of Ladies' Walk and sank to her knees. At least she was out of sight. Through a gap in the bushes she could see that the couple had turned into Ladies' Walk, and she could hear the voices distinctly. One was high and commanding: Lady Mungo! She pricked up her ears.

"It was really stupid of me to have taken the painting from the dining room. But I'd had such a shock," Lady Mungo was saying. "With hindsight, I see taking it was unnecessary. And now it's missing."

"You worry too much, Mother," came the smooth voice of Percy. "What if that wretched thing is missing. One of the servants took it—that's as plain as a pikestaff."

"But suppose it turns up? I had planned to have it destroyed. That's the reason I had it put in the attics. A small fire started in a bucket—the way Fowler gets rid of records, get him to show you how he does it—could easily have been started and then put out with no damage to the castle. And there would have been proof of its destruction. One of the servants could have been blamed."

"But even if it does turn up, what about it? Nobody can put two and two together."

"I've something else on my mind. Those paupers we sent to Canada didn't go at all. At roll call the

party was five short. And Fowler has heard say that a
family by the name of Madden was admitted to the
workhouse."

"But how can that be? Thomas would have reported to you if that had happened. It must be a different family."

"I don't trust those servants. They're all in league
together against us."

Just as they were passing her, Emma saw to her
horror that one of the apples she had gathered in her
apron had rolled out and landed just in front of
Percy. Now she was in for it!

But Percy just picked up the apple, rubbed it,
and sank his teeth into its juicy ripeness. Lady

Mungo was too preoccupied to have even noticed the incident.

"In the meanwhile, I'll get Fowler to check at the workhouse about the Maddens. I really won't rest easy until the agent in Grosse Ile confirms they have arrived. I hope their stay won't be long—they say thousands have died there of the fever."

"Mother, do you think you're wise trusting Fowler?"

"Percy, at times I think you're as dense as your father. How could I have dealt with the Maddens without Fowler? And all the servants I've gotten rid of and the cuts I've made? He handles all the financial details and can divert the money to us."

"Suppose he talks and confesses he helped us to defraud the estate?"

"And implicate himself? He won't."

"Still, I wouldn't trust him too far."

"Depend on it, I won't. What a nuisance that the Clifdens seem to have decided to come back—though I've had no word from them yet. I thought they'd stay away for a couple of years. Maybe old Staunton is ailing."

"Coming home to die? Whether he does or not, all's well as long as he doesn't father another child."

"Unlikely, after all these years. . . . I think we'll go in. It's getting cold . . ."

The voices drifted away. When they were well out of earshot, Emma got to her feet, brushed down her skirt, and gathered up the rest of the apples. She would have to act quickly. Fowler would shortly be going over to the workhouse—where he would find out that Mrs. Madden had died and her two daughters had disappeared. Soon he would be combing the estate. She would have to go to the attics immediately and talk to Bridie. But what excuse could she give? As she pushed her hair back up under her cap, an idea struck her. She took off her cap and threw it into the bushes.

She raced back to the kitchen, put the apples on the table, and said to Mrs. Burke, "I would have brought more, but I only had my apron to carry them in. I had no cap."

"Where's your cap?"

"I don't know. I think I must have lost it when we were searching the attics yesterday."

"Were you not wearing it this morning? I could have sworn you were."

As Emma shook her head, she saw Nancy give her a sharp glance.

"Well, off you go and get it. On the double. Lady Muck will have a fit if she comes into the kitchen and finds you with hair all over the place like a gypsy."

Emma ran up the winding servants' stairs, through the green baize door on the third floor, then along the corridor of servants' bedrooms to the oak door that led to the attics. She pushed it open and took the stairs two at a time, hoping she wouldn't meet any strange denizens of that top story. As she stood in the center of the corridor, trying to establish exactly where she had seen the old woman, she heard a creaking sound, like a door being shut.

Someone was coming up the stairs. Soon he or she would see her. And there was no escape. Or at least not back the way she had come.

She stood there, heart thumping. Who could it be?

The Little Dog

"Who's there?" said a voice from the top of the stairs. She recognized the voice instantly. It was Percy.

"I didn't hear anything," said a deeper voice. Fowler!

In panic, Emma ran a few yards, then stopped where she had seen the old woman pause. She shrank back into the shadows, hoping that the curtain hanging halfway down the corridor would hide her.

"In case of an emergency," Fowler went on, "get rid of everything. It's safe here. Too many snoopers around the stable yard. This room is the best. Come in and I'll show you what to do."

There was the sound of a door being closed. "Really," thought Emma to herself, "I'm getting to be a champion eavesdropper. But I can't go back up the corridor, that's certain. I'll have to find the priest's hole."

She turned the door knob of the last room very quietly and slipped in. Hastily she looked around her. Old furniture, bundles of frayed curtains, trunks — the same mixture as before. Didn't they ever throw anything out? She went all around the walls, pushing and probing, but there wasn't an opening anywhere. Sally must have been mistaken. About to give up in despair, she nearly knocked over an old washstand

and just saved it from falling with a crash. Just as well she hadn't banged into that massive old chest, with its hideous carving of two animals fighting on front, that stood against one wall. She stared at the chest, then had a sudden brainwave. Could the priest's hole be behind it? She tugged at it but nothing happened. It was immovable. It was part of the wall!

She had tried to open it before when the old woman had disappeared, and had given up. Now she was certain it *could* be opened. It seemed to be locked and there was no key, but she kept exploring the surface. Then a pressure on the molding swung it open slightly. She crept in and ran her hand over the wall at the back of the chest, pressing it bit by bit. At first there was nothing. Then a tiny opening. Then the wall seemed to recede. She was looking into a small room with rough unplastered walls. The priest's hole! And through the opening in the wall facing her, she could see stairs leading down into the darkness.

In her excitement at finding the priest's hole, Emma had almost forgotten what she was searching for. Bridie and Paddy! But there was nobody in the room, though on the floor lay an old mattress, bed-clothes, even a plate that should have been stacked on the dresser in the kitchen. Bridie and Paddy *had* been there. Where had they gone? Had they been discovered? Were they now under armed guard on their way back to Galway and forced emigration?

With a sick sense of disappointment, she looked

around before going to the stairs. Then she tripped over something. A gilded frame. Empty. The painting that had once been there had been taken out. At the base of the frame was an inscription: Lady Alicia Lambert.

The secret staircase was steep and circular with jagged uneven steps, and Emma had to go down very carefully, keeping a hand on the rough walls. At the end was a small door that opened when she tugged hard. Cautiously she crept out, blinking in the sunshine. She was in a small courtyard, with the kitchen wing to her right. When she emerged, the curtain of heavy ivy, which almost hid the door, fell back into place. Only a very sharp eye would discover the entrance behind all the growth.

She had lost all sense of time. How long had she been away? Was the sun ascending or descending? She knew she should get her cap and go back to the kitchen immediately. But she also realized she had to see Sally and warn her about Fowler.

"There will probably be trouble," she thought, "but I just have to go to Sally." She retrieved her cap and set off down the path that led to the oak tree, hoping Sally and Maria would be there.

They were and came down when they heard Emma call.

"Bridie and Paddy were in the priest's hole,"

Emma said. "But they've gone now. What do you think could have happened? Could they have been found? By Fowler?"

Sally shook her head. "That's impossible. But it's all very strange. And how annoying that, just when you found their hiding place, they've disappeared again. You'll have to go back to O'Flaherty."

"There's something even stranger," said Emma, when she had finished recounting the conversation she had overheard between Lady Mungo and Percy. "Why was she so determined to have your family evicted and sent away?"

"I suppose it was because Da died and we were just a set of useless mouths, begging for food."

"Lady Mungo?" said Maria, who had been sitting quietly beside them, making a daisy chain. "She has such a nice little dog."

Sally stared at her in amazement. "But you don't know her. You never saw her in your life."

"I did," said Maria timidly. Then her face crinkled slightly. "You won't be cross with me?"

"No," said Sally, giving her a hug. "No one is going to be cross with you. Just tell us what happened."

"Once Ma and I were walking in the woods when a carriage came by. We stepped back into the trees so that the people in it wouldn't see us. Ma said to me afterward, 'That's Lady Mungo Lambert. Never let

her see you.' She didn't say why, but I was always afraid in case I would meet her. Then one day . . . ," she paused a little, then went on, "I found a wee dog. It was caught in some brambles. I got it out, and next thing, Lady Mungo was there. She looked at me for a long time, then took the dog and went away. I didn't tell Ma. I knew she would be cross. I remember it so well because of the dog." She looked wistful. "I'd love to have one like it."

"When did this happen?"

"It . . . it was the day before they came and knocked our home down."

Sally and Emma looked at each other, and then at Maria. Maria with her innocent blue eyes and tousled fair hair. Each was thinking the same thought. Was Maria the real reason why the Maddens had been evicted from the Moylough estate? And what had Lady Mungo seen in Maria that made her such a threat?

Bridie's Story

The Clifdens did not come back that day. Even Mrs. Burke's high good humor of the morning evaporated as the evening wore on. She hadn't even commented on Emma's lengthy search for her cap; she just told her to wash the floor again.

It was a gloomy evening. There was no lingering sunset, and no one suggested going for a walk in the orchard. Darkness set in early.

"Evening's closing in already." Mrs. Burke heaved a sigh. "And there's going to be a storm. I can feel it in my bones. We're in for an equinoctial gale, mark my words."

"Too early for one," remarked Agnes.

Mrs. Burke just looked at her and went on drinking her tea. "Reminds me of the evening poor old Lord Clifden—that's the old earl, God rest his soul—died. There was this darkness and this deathly stillness. Then the moon came up, a full moon. I had to bring him up some broth, and when I was coming down the stairs I looked out through that big window at the back overlooking the lawns. I'll never forget what I saw . . ." She blessed herself. "I could see over the park, and there they were. Deer. Hundreds of them. They came all around the castle and just stayed there."

"What's so odd about that?" asked Agnes. "There are always deer in the park."

"Not like these. They were ghostly white and didn't make a sound. They were the Clifden deer. They appear when the earl dies or is about to die. There's an old poem about it. Lord bless me. I haven't thought about it in years. I've forgotten the half of it:

> My love dwelt in a northern land,
> A gray tower in a forest green.
>
> ★
>
> I knew not that my love was lorn,
> I knew not that he wounded lay.
> Then in the night there came the deer.
> All through the night they came,
> Pale, silver deer on silent feet,
> And circled round the castle walls.
>
> ★
>
> The grass above his grave is green,
> His heart is colder than a stone.

"I remember the mourning," said Agnes, who had taken out her knitting. "Such quantities of everything. Forty-four yards of linen at five shillings and five pence a yard, a hundred and sixty-six yards at two shillings and eight pence halfpenny a yard, twenty yards of muslin, forty-six hat bands, a hundred and forty-four pairs of gloves, thirty cloaks, and a hundred and fifty yards of ribbon. Not to mention black cloth and stockings, jet buttons, and material for black drapings."

"Yes, the local business did well out of it."

After that, the talk was relentlessly of death and disaster, and as the rising wind moaned around the windows and rattled the doors, Emma wished it were morning, so that she'd be rid of this gloomy evening and could find out where Paddy and Bridie were.

But there was to be no trip to the kitchen yard next morning. Emma woke to the sound of heavy rain as a westerly gale beat on the windowpanes and tore through the trees, bending and breaking branches and scattering leaves and fruits and berries. When Annie attempted to open the passage door, a torrent of water rushed through and it took them all their strength to get it closed again.

"Well, the Clifdens certainly aren't coming home today," sighed Mrs. Burke. "They'll stay put until to-morrow, wherever they are."

"Or the day after," said Agnes. "These storms sometimes take a few days to blow out."

But, unexpectedly, it cleared in the late afternoon, and the day was soft and smiling again. Emma was only too delighted to be sent out to the kitchen yard with vegetables for the soup.

"Let's get a few apples," said Annie when they had dumped their buckets.

"You do. I'll be along in a minute," said Emma. She went into the small house where O'Flaherty lived and knocked at the door. He smiled as he came out.

"Now, let me guess. You want to know about your two friends, the ones you couldn't find."

"How did you know?"

He smiled mysteriously. "There are a lot of things I know. And only tell to the right people."

"I'm a right person," said Emma, wishing he would get to the point before they were interrupted. "You must tell me. Where are Paddy and Bridie? I must know. It's really important."

"Paddy you won't find—he's a little distance away. But Bridie is here. She couldn't come out of hiding until she knew for certain the Clifdens were coming home."

"Where is she?"

"Now that's the odd thing. You're looking for her . . . and she's looking for you."

"For me?"

"The two you are with. Where are they?"

"Can I trust you?"

"Bridie could."

"You know the old oak tree beyond the orchard?" O'Flaherty nodded. "Follow the path until you come to the bog. There's a small scalp there."

"Ah, where the Kellys were."

As Emma turned to go away, he said, "Bridie left something here. Something you might be interested in seeing."

She followed him into the dark interior and up a

rickety staircase to the loft above. There he pointed to
a roll that was wrapped in old curtaining.

"Open it."

Emma carefully unwound the curtain and found
herself looking at a painting. A portrait of a young girl
with long blond hair, dressed in pale blue, a pink
rosebud nestled in her lace collar.

She was looking at Maria!

"Bridie had to leave the frame behind her when
she left the priest's hole."

The frame! Lady Alicia Lambert!

In a blinding flash it came to her.

Emma didn't go back to the kitchen. She raced off
through the wet grass, down the now familiar path-
way, to the oak tree. But there was no answering call
when she gave the signal. Then it occurred to her that
Sally and Maria wouldn't have been at the oak tree
through that frightful storm. They would be at the
scalp.

"I can't go back now," she thought as she continued on through the forest to the edge of the bog.

How things had changed since the day they had
arrived at the castle. Then it was summer, even though
the first faint color was beginning to creep into the
trees; now it was autumn, with strewn branches, even
parts of tree trunks, on the ground, and dead leaves
everywhere.

Sally was at the scalp.

"I thought I'd missed you," said Emma. "I've wonderful news. Bridie is here. And she's looking for you. O'Flaherty told me. He knew where she was all along. And old Liza must have been bringing her food. He knows where Paddy is too. And I've something else to tell you . . ."

At that moment they heard a noise outside. Emma and Sally froze into silence, not daring to move. A soft voice called, "Sally!" Then a tall, pleasant-faced woman came into the interior.

"Bridie!" shouted Sally, throwing herself into her arms. "Where have you been all the time? We looked everywhere for you."

"I was hiding. Until I knew for sure the Clifdens

were coming back, I had to. But with Fowler and Percy snooping around all the time and the storm yesterday and today, this is the first chance I've had to look for you."

Emma turned to Bridie. "I found the priest's hole, but you weren't there."

"So it was you!" Bridie laughed. "I heard someone rummaging around in the room and I thought it was Percy. So I got out through the stairs and hid in the old scullery until it was dark. Then I went to O'Flaherty, who hid me upstairs. I was terrified of being discovered—he told me Lady Mungo had ordered a thorough search of the castle grounds. Then, luckily, the storm came . . ."

"Tell me quickly," said Sally, tugging at Bridie's sleeve. "What was it Ma wanted you to tell me? About Maria. What is it?"

"That Maria is not Maria at all," said Emma quietly. "She is Lady Charlotte Lambert, daughter of Lord and Lady Clifden."

"How on earth did you guess?" asked Bridie.

"Just now. When I saw the portrait in O'Flaherty's house."

"What portrait?" Sally sounded puzzled.

"We'll come to that later," said Bridie. "Just let me tell my story." She sat down on the one small stool in the scalp and the other two squatted on the ground.

"As you know, the Clifdens were married quite a few years before there was a sign of a child. Then, happily, Lady Clifden became pregnant. They were so delighted. A son, or a daughter, to inherit the title and the estate. Then, one autumn day, when they were walking in the woods, Her Ladyship went into early labor.

"Lord Clifden was beside himself. He helped her to your cabin," she nodded at Sally, "which was the nearest place—and rushed off to get the carriage and send for the doctor. Your father wasn't there, but your mother was. She'd had a baby the day before. You must have been there too."

"I vaguely remember the fuss," said Sally, "but I was only six. All I clearly remember was Ma telling me to go out and play."

"But before Lord Clifden got back with the doctor and Mrs. MacWilliams, the housekeeper, the baby was born. Your mother said it was only when she was wrapping the child that the anger hit her. There was Her Ladyship, dressed in all her finery, knowing nothing but luxury, and this tiny baby, so puny she did not think it would live the night, who would grow up in that same privileged world. And there was her own new baby, Maria, healthy and vigorous, who would only know a life of poverty and uncertainty. She told me she didn't know what came over her but she said to herself, 'Why should it be this way?' Before she had time to change her mind, she picked up Maria and placed her in Lady Clifden's arms— and put the newborn baby in Maria's box.

"Afterward your mother thought someone would surely notice what had been done, that someone would realize that the 'newborn' baby was too well-developed for a premature baby. The substitution would be discovered, and the truth would be known. But when Lord Clifden arrived back with the doctor and the housekeeper, all the concern was for Lady Clifden, who was almost unconscious. Her color was bad, her pulse barely there. Mother and baby were wrapped in shawls and brought to the castle. Then the doctor was summoned urgently to Pennyfield Hall, where Lady Garville had been thrown from her horse. So no one really examined the baby, except to give thanks that in spite of being premature it seemed healthy and hearty. Indeed Lord Clifden thanked your mother for her expert help in assisting the birth and gave her a guinea.

"The real Clifden heir somehow survived. From a tiny sickly baby she grew into a lovely girl. She had long fair hair, and every time your mother looked at her she could see Clifden written all over her. 'She's just like the portrait of Lady Alicia in the dining room,' she told me. That's why she was so careful not to let anyone from the castle see her. The Madden baby, now called Lady Charlotte, also grew into a healthy happy child, but she was not at all like either Lord or Lady Clifden. They tried to find a resemblance somewhere and thought they traced it back to an aunt of Lady Clifden's, who had had dark hair.

Old Alicia, Lord Clifden's aunt, was concerned that Lady Charlotte didn't have the butterfly mark, but Lord Clifden told her not to be so silly—that birthmarks don't always appear."

"The what?" asked Sally.

"The butterfly mark. It's a distinctive little birthmark—you might almost imagine it was a butterfly—that nearly all the Clifdens have on their right shoulder."

"Go on," said Sally.

"Your mother really lived through hell all those years. She was terrified of what she had done but thought it was impossible to undo the damage. And when the Clifden heir, brought up as Maria Madden, the child she was so sure would die, survived, she knew she was guilty of depriving her of the life and inheritance she should have had. Then Lady Charlotte, your mother's real child, died. Your mother was beside herself and said that Charlotte's death and your father's at the same time and of the same fever were a judgment on her for what she had done.

"You may wonder why she didn't immediately go to Lord and Lady Clifden and confess what she had done—after all, it would have been great news for them that their real daughter was alive. She did try, after the funeral, but she was not allowed to see the Clifdens. In any case, they left Moylough a few days after Charlotte's death. At that stage how could she have told Lady Mungo that Percy was not the heir? It would have meant transportation for herself and the workhouse for Sally. Indeed, that's almost what happened, though in different circumstances."

"How did you get to know all this?" asked Sally.

"As you know, Lady Mungo decided to get rid of tenants, to give them assisted passage to Canada. There was really no choice in the matter. Some didn't mind. They felt that they had nothing to gain by staying here and perhaps things would be better in a new land. Your family wasn't on the original list—I suppose because your dad, Hughie, was dead and your parents weren't on the rent roll. Then Lady Mungo seemed to make a last-minute decision about your family. Your mother sent an urgent message for me to come and see her. It was then—just a few short days ago—that she told me the whole story. She was in despair, said she couldn't go to Canada, that Maria would have to have her rightful inheritance but she didn't know what to do about it.

"At first we couldn't see any solution. But Mrs. Burke had told me privately—she'd heard it from Jamie—that the Clifdens were in Dublin, so we decided Paddy, who was with me, would go to Dublin and tell Lord Clifden he must return urgently. Your family would have to go on to Canada—where would you have lived if you had come back here? Your cabin was in ruins. I was to pretend to go with the emigrants, then disappear, and come back here and hide until the Clifdens got back. Then I could tell them the whole story.

"At the back of my mind was the idea that maybe the emigrant ship wouldn't have left by the time the Clifdens got to Moylough—those ships are often a couple of weeks late in leaving. At the worse, I knew Lord Clifden could find your family in Grosse Ile."

"Did Paddy tell Lord Clifden about Maria?"

"No. We were afraid if he did, the Clifdens would think it a cruel hoax and refuse to come back. He was just to say that a lot of tenants had been sent away and ask the Clifdens to come back to Moylough urgently. Indeed, Lord Clifden may already have heard stories of what was happening on the estate."

"How did you know about the priest's hole?" asked Emma.

"O'Flaherty. I went straight to him. He knew about it. The castle was an old O'Flaherty keep."

"So you were on your own all those days," said Sally.

"It wasn't too bad. Liza brought me food. And I had company." She laughed. "Lady Alicia Lambert! We knew Lady Mungo had put the painting into the attics. I was sure she was planning to have it disappear altogether. I found it and took it to the priest's hole with me. When I left there, I removed the frame to make it easier to hide. It should be proof of Maria's ancestry."

"We have better proof than that," said Sally. "Maria has the butterfly mark on her shoulder. I often wondered what it was. I thought it was a faint skin mark and would go away."

"Where is Maria?" asked Bridie.

"Outside. She wanted to get out and play all morning but she couldn't on account of the storm. So just before you came in, I let her out and told her not to go far or make any noise. I'll call her," she said, running out.

When she returned she was ashen faced. "I can't find her!"

They went outside and began to search the area around the scalp. But there was no trace of Maria.

"Fowler!" cried Emma. "He must have come across her. And he would have been looking for her."

"They'll spirit her away," said Sally in dejection, "and she'll never be found again. I've failed in my promise to Ma. I should never have let Maria out on her own. It's all my fault."

"Nobody can blame you," said Emma, putting her arm around Sally. "You are so good to her."

"Let's go back to the castle," said Bridie. "Maybe someone has seen her. We must find her before the Clifdens return."

"The oak tree," shouted Sally suddenly. "Maybe that's where she is."

Emma flew after her and they soon reached the clearing and the tree. Sally gave the wood pigeon call but there was no reply. Then a face peered through the leaves.

"It's Maria!" cried Sally. "You're safe now. Come on down."

Maria clambered down. She had been crying and ran to Sally. "I thought you'd never come. Don't be cross with me. I went a little way into the bog. There were some beautiful red berries on a bush there and I wanted to pick some for you. Then I heard the sound of a horse and saw a big black horse and a man with a black mustache."

"Fowler!" said Emma.

"He shouted at me and told me to stay where I was, that he wanted to bring me up to the castle. I was terrified. I ran and ran into the forest. He would have caught me, but the horse couldn't get through the trees as quickly as I could. I made for the oak tree and climbed up. I knew he hadn't seen me, and soon after I heard the sound of the horse galloping away. And I'm cold and wet and hungry . . ."

"Well, you won't be for much longer," promised Sally.

Good-Byes

The acrid smell of smoke reached their nostrils as they approached the castle.

"Burning leaves already?" thought Emma, bewildered that anyone would have time for gardening after the dramatic story of life and death they'd just been told. Then she saw smoke pouring out of one of the narrow windows on the attic floor.

In the front courtyard, all was confusion. Hannah and Nancy were rushing about with buckets of water, futile though that was. Mrs. Burke was there too, wringing her hands. Annie and Agnes were in a group looking upward.

"What happened?" asked Emma.

"Someone started a fire in the attics," moaned Mrs. Burke. "MacGregor and O'Flaherty are up there trying to put it out. They'll all be burnt to death. And the castle will go up in smoke."

"Nonsense, it's only a small fire," said Bridie. "I'm sure they'll have gotten it in time."

Just then there was the sound of carriage wheels, and up the avenue came a carriage with two outriders. It stopped at the courtyard gates, and Lord Clifden stepped out.

"What's all this?" he asked.

"A small fire in one of the attic rooms," said Lady Mungo smoothly, emerging through the front door. "Started maliciously. By this wretched girl." She walked over to the cluster of servants and caught Emma by the shoulder. "Don't deny it, girl."

"And how could she have started it?" asked Mrs. Burke. "Wasn't she here with all of us?"

"I saw her coming into the courtyard just now," said Lady Mungo. "She started the fire, then came down the servants' stairs and only joined you a minute or so ago."

Bridie stepped forward. "She was with me for the past hour."

Lady Mungo gave Bridie an angry look. "And where did you appear from? Another conspiracy!"

"What's all this about?" His Lordship sounded bewildered. "And who is this?" pointing to Emma.

"A scullery maid. I was about to give her notice because of insubordination, and then she goes and does this."

"She's lying," cried Emma, appealing to Lord Clifden. "She wants to have me sent away because I know the truth."

"The truth about what?"

"Don't listen to the ravings of a scullery maid. Let me send her on her way."

"It's too late now," said Emma. "The truth will have to be told."

"About what?" asked Lord Clifden.

"Your daughter, Charlotte."

A look of pain crossed his thin face. "My daughter is dead." He was about to turn away when Emma cried, "Bridie, get Maria."

Bridie drew Maria into the sunlit courtyard and turned her to face Lord and Lady Clifden, who had just joined her husband.

"Does she remind you of anyone?" asked Emma.

"She's the image of my aunt Alicia when she was a child. But how can that be?"

"Sir, it's because her real name is Charlotte, and she is your daughter."

Lady Clifden was looking at Maria as if she had seen a ghost. "Can it really be true?" she whispered.

"Don't believe a word that girl is saying. It's all lies. Horrible lies to upset you and Lord Clifden," said Lady Mungo.

"Bridie can tell you the whole truth. Mary Madden told her the story of how the babies were switched at birth."

"It's such a strange story that I don't think I'm taking it all in," said Lord Clifden. "Let us change our clothes and we'll meet in Lady Clifden's sitting room in a little while."

Just then MacGregor and O'Flaherty emerged from the house, smoke stained and disheveled, to announce that the fire was under control. O'Flaherty was grasping Percy in an iron grip.

"He was trying to start a fire in one of the rooms in the attics. He had papers with him."

Emma, who was standing near Lady Mungo, heard her sudden intake of breath and her almost inaudible, "Fool, you stupid young fool!"

Lord Clifden looked from Lady Mungo to Percy. "You'd better come too. I think you have some explaining to do."

As Emma turned to go back to the kitchen, she saw Lady Clifden take Maria by the hand and lead her into the castle.

"She knows, she knows!" she thought exultantly.

"They won't want me," said Sally when Emma, Bridie, and Paddy, who had returned with the Clifdens, got the summons to go upstairs.

"They'll want you," said Emma firmly. "Or will, when they hear the whole story. And Maria will be asking where you are. So you have to come now. If you don't, I'll only be sent to fetch you. And I've had enough stairs for a lifetime."

"You're impossible," Sally said, giving her a dig, but Emma was relieved to see a smile break over her face.

As they went up the servants' stairs, Emma remembered the first time she had climbed them to go up to the attics. How much had happened since then. Now her commitment was almost at an end and she could go home. Smiling, she thought to herself that she had forgotten to ask Sally if she still had the ring. But of course Sally had it.

They went through the first green baize door into a corridor lined with somber portraits in heavy gold frames. The high ceiling was vaulted and stags' heads stared at them solemnly as they passed. At one point they could see the massive front door, but Bridie turned up the wide mahogany staircase. She stopped at a dark-paneled door and knocked.

"Come in," said a soft voice.

The room was small and cozy, light streaming through tall windows. Lady Clifden was sitting on a low curved chair, her long black dress falling in graceful folds to the floor. Maria was seated on a low stool by her side, and from time to time Lady Clifden reached down to pat her shoulder as if to make sure she was still there. When she saw Sally, Maria jumped up and rushed over to her.

"Oh, Sally, where have you been? Look, they took away my old clothes and got me these lovely new ones."

Both Lord and Lady Clifden smiled, and then Lord Clifden said, "Bridie, I think you have something to tell us."

Bridie began to speak, haltingly at first, then more fluently, as she recounted the strange episode of Charlotte's birth.

When Bridie had finished, Lady Clifden said in a sad voice, "All those years. Surely Mrs. Madden

could have come and told me. She could have trusted
me."

"She'd had a very hard life. She was an orphan
herself. I think that was really why she wanted her
baby to have a better chance in life. She felt she
couldn't trust anyone. And she was afraid."

"Afraid of what?"

"She thought she would have been transported
and Sally put in the workhouse."

"How can you believe a word of this rigmarole?"
said Lady Mungo, unable to restrain herself any
longer. "They're all in it. It's a plot to deprive Percy
of his rightful inheritance."

"Rightful!" Lord Clifden gave a grim smile.

"I didn't mean it like that," replied Lady Mungo in honeyed tones. "You know that. Of course you have very many years ahead of you."

"Bridie is telling the truth and you know it," put in Emma, addressing herself to Lady Mungo. "You were the one who ordered the eviction of the Maddens. And I know why. You saw Maria in the woods and could see the family resemblance."

"Nonsense, I thought they would have a better life in Canada. What were they to do after Hughie Madden died? Fowler agreed with me and he arranged it." She turned to Lord Clifden. "You weren't here, so someone had to make decisions."

"I gather a great many decisions were made," said Lord Clifden. "Fowler will have to account for his part in all of them."

"I still don't understand how Lady Mungo connected Maria with the painting," said Lady Clifden.

"I think I can answer that," said Bridie. "You remember Mrs. MacWilliams who used to be housekeeper here—she went with Lord Clifden to the cabin to get the baby after it was born. There was such fuss and confusion that nobody really examined the baby— the doctor was called away as soon as he got to the castle. But Mrs. MacWilliams did. She never said a word then, but sometimes, when she'd had a drop or two, she would say, 'The Clifden baby. It wasn't a right baby.' Nobody thought anything of it, except that she was referring to the birthmark. You probably haven't heard, but Mrs. MacWilliams died last week—she never got over the fever she caught in February. When she was dying she sent for Fowler. Maybe she told him of her suspicions. He would have told Lady Mungo immediately. So she went to the Madden cabin to see Maria for herself. When she saw Maria she must have been shattered at the likeness to Lady Alicia. She knew then that Maria was the heir."

"You don't need the portrait—which, by the way, O'Flaherty has safely hidden," put in Emma. "There is something else. Something even Lady Mungo can't explain away. Maria has the Clifden birthmark."

Emma undid the buttons at the neck of Maria's dress and showed the Clifdens the small butterfly-shaped mark on Maria's shoulder.

Lord and Lady Clifden spoke quietly together for a few moments. Then he spoke: "Emily, I have to say I have never liked you. I thought poor Mungo married beneath him. Not in birth or family but in character. And so it turned out. You're nothing but a grasping creature and your son—I won't call him my nephew—is as bad. You are to leave here and never return. And, depend on it, Percy will never see a penny of my money. Of course, I won't cut you off as you would have cut off Maria. I'll send you sufficient to live on. All we can hope is that you become a reformed character."

As Lady Mungo and her son were escorted from the room, Lord Clifden turned to Sally. "You are a brave girl. Even though you didn't know the full story, you carried out your mother's dying wish and brought Maria here. You did everything you could to try to unravel the mystery."

"I'm sorry it all happened," mumbled Sally.

"You are not to blame for your mother's act. God knows, I can well understand the temptation she had. And you too have suffered. Both your parents are dead and you have just learned of the death of the sister you never knew. We loved her dearly. Now we must put the past behind us and look forward to a happier future. Maria will, of course, come to live with us."

"Sally, too," said Maria. "I must have Sally."

Lord and Lady Clifden both smiled as Lady Clifden said, "But of course. Sally will stay with us as your companion and . . . sister. You may not be blood sisters, but you will always think of one another as that."

"What about you, Emma?" asked Lord Clifden.

"I have relations," said Emma. "I must go back to them. I have stayed too long as it is."

"Can we help you?" Lady Clifden asked. "Paddy or Hogan will take you anywhere you want to go."

"No thanks," replied Emma. "It's really not too far from here. I'd rather go back on my own."

Lord Clifden looked at her keenly. "As you wish, my dear."

"Can Sally and Maria walk a little of the way with me?"

"Of course, but do hurry back, girls," said Lady Clifden.

In the kitchen courtyard, O'Flaherty was loading turf and logs into big baskets. "I must say good-bye to him," Emma told Sally. "Wait for me at the oak tree."

"Is it really true, Mr. O'Flaherty," she asked him, "that this castle once belonged to your family?"

"The oldest part of it—with the priest's hole. It was a very primitive castle then."

"Don't you resent working here as a servant in what should be your property?"

"Not mine alone. There are hordes of O'Flahertys. But we're still around, those of us who weren't sent to the West Indies. We're laborers, servants, tenants. We're biding our time. Waiting in the forest for the foreigner to go so that we'll come into our own again."

"Unlikely," thought Emma, holding out her hand. "Thanks for everything. If it hadn't been for you I don't know what would have happened."

"You did a fair share of bringing about the ending yourself."

"Mr. O'Flaherty, that's the nicest thing anyone has ever said to me."

She bypassed the kitchen door, feeling a little mean about not saying good-bye to Mrs. Burke and Nancy and Annie. But with preparations for the homecoming dinner under way she knew she would have found it very hard to get away without answering some awkward questions. "I'll get Sally to say good-bye for me," she thought.

When she joined Sally and Maria, Sally said curiously, "Where exactly are you going? You said near here. Where? And why must you go home now?"

"Sally, you mustn't ask me any questions. . . . Now, can I have my ring back?"

Sally put her hand into a little pouch around her neck and gave a cry. "It's missing! It's gone!" Then seeing Emma's horrified face, she burst out laughing. "I'm only joking. Here it is. When you're gone, Maria will spend hours wondering why it was so important to you."

"Sally, tell her," urged Maria.

"Emma, Maria and I want to give you something special. Lady Clifden said she would help. Will you come back in a few days for it?"

"I'm not so sure I'll be able to come back," Emma said unsteadily. "But thank you. It was nice of you to think of me."

"But it doesn't seem right. You've been so good to us. Had it not been for you, Maria would never have known her real parents. I'll tell you what. We'll leave your present in the oak tree. So if we're not here when you come back, you can still get it. Promise you'll come back."

Emma was silent for a moment, knowing she could never explain exactly what going home meant to her. How could they possibly understand? Then seeing the two anxious faces before her, she said, "I'll come back for your present. I promise."

"Will we walk another part of the way with you?" asked Sally.

"No, I have to carry on alone from here," said Emma, and as she gave them a hug Sally said tearfully, "We could never have succeeded without you. We'll miss you."

Emma stood and sadly watched until her friends were out of sight, and then she sat beneath the oak tree. Her eyes were bright with tears when she took the ruby ring from her pocket and, slipping it on her finger, tried to remember how she had made her wish before. Then it came back to her; she had been twisting the ring. So, turning it round and round, she said in a whisper, "I wish I was back in Lucy McLaughlin's room again."

Leaning against the tree trunk, she grew sleepy as she listened to the soft rustling of the leaves above and wondered dreamily if it was late because the wood had become darker. Then suddenly there was nothing. Everything had turned to blackness.

The Butterfly Brooch

Emma sat up suddenly and rubbed her eyes. She must have fallen asleep. Her book lay open on the floor. She had been reading *Jane Eyre* but she had been so upset that she couldn't concentrate. Jean and Paul thought she was selfish and self-centered, probably Lucy and David did too. She had decided she wanted to do something good and unselfish for someone. She had put on Lucy's ruby ring and she had had such a peculiar dream. Parts of it were quite frightening.

The sound of voices and the closing of the front door indicated that Lucy and David were back. Returning the ring to its box, Emma ran down the stairs and greeted them. "I'm sorry I didn't go with you. Maybe we can go tomorrow, if Dad doesn't come."

After a cheerful tea, with everyone talking thirteen to the dozen, Emma said, "Let me help with the washing up—I'll do the saucepan."

"Scrambled eggs? Are you sure?" asked Jean in some surprise.

"Don't worry, I'm a dab hand at saucepans. Leave it to me."

As she took the saucepan, Emma looked at her

hands. She had expected them to be red and sore from the silver sand, but they were the same as always. "Look, shining!" she said, holding the saucepan up for inspection. "Now, what does anyone want to do?"

Lucy and David looked at one another in surprise. "We thought of Scrabble," said Lucy tentatively, "but would you prefer to do anything else?"

"Scrabble sounds just fine." Soon they were having a noisy game, which ended with Emma congratulating Lucy on winning.

Next morning, her father phoned.

"I wanted to be the first to wish you a happy birthday," he said.

"Thanks, Dad," said Emma, glad to hear his voice again. "How is Maeve?"

"Fine, just fine. The tests are all right but the doctors want to keep her in another day. So I'll come up for you tomorrow. Is that all right?"

"Great, Dad. See you tomorrow," said Emma happily, and went to tell Jean the news.

Jean and Paul gave her a Boyzone CD for her birthday, and Lucy and David treated her to a pizza at Fredo's Pizza Parlor, where she had the biggest pepperoni pizza ever. Then they went swimming and played video games after tea.

As she was going to bed that night, David said, "When are you coming again?"

"I don't know, maybe next holidays. If you'll have me?" said Emma.

"Any time. Right, Lucy?"

"Right," agreed Lucy with a laugh.

Emma was packed and ready the following morning when her dad arrived, and after chatting with Jean and Paul they said good-bye and set out for Galway. There was a traffic diversion outside Tuam and farther on they came across a crowd of protesters crossing the street of a small village.

"I wonder what they're protesting now. It's always something these days," Rory muttered as he increased speed again outside the village.

Helen was at home when they arrived and Emma opened her presents. One was a personal CD player.

"Super!" said Emma. "Just what I always wanted." Her other present was a book token.

Maeve was asleep in her cot when they went in to see her, but she opened her eyes when they came in. Her tousled fair hair reminded Emma of Maria and with a pang of remembrance she scooped her into her arms and cuddled her.

"Aren't I lucky to have a baby sister!"

Later in bed as she looked around at the familiar objects in the room, she thought of the bedroom in Moylough Castle. She could see every object, from the iron bedstead to the washbasin to the jug with a chip in it. And before that there had been the awful dormitory in the workhouse. It all seemed so real.

Surely it couldn't have been just a dream. As she drifted off to sleep, she was thinking of Sally and Maria and she wondered what present they would have given her.

A new school term temporarily banished Sally and Maria from Emma's mind. Then one evening, when she was in the sitting room looking after Maeve while Helen was preparing supper, an item on *Newsround* caught her attention and she turned up the volume to hear the announcer.

"The angry residents of Castlebridge are continuing their protests over the proposed new motorway planned for the area, as this would mean the destruction of ancient woods, which are part of the estate once belonging to Moylough Castle. The castle has been unoccupied since a fire destroyed part of the building in 1922 and the owner, the Countess of Clifden, and her son went to live in England. The woods have remained a great attraction to visitors over the years and residents are angry at the planners' lack of interest in preserving them."

Emma sat spellbound as the cameras showed the gates of Moylough Castle and part of the woods.

So it was not just a dream. It had really happened. Her mind was racing as the report closed with a shot of the avenue, now very overgrown. She would have to go there—and luckily tomorrow was a Saturday so there was no school. Castlebridge was not too far from Galway, and she could get a bus.

She slept little that night as she tried to plan the

day ahead. She would leave early. And she wouldn't
tell Dad or Helen her exact plan. They might only
worry. Anyway, how could you explain a dream that
had turned out to be real after all?

Next morning she announced, "I want to go into
town today. I might go to the library and to Kenny's
bookshop. I still have my book token. I probably
won't be home until evening."

"What are you going to buy?" asked Helen.

"Hardiman's *History of the Town and County of
Galway,* if I can get it."

"Sounds a bit ponderous," said her father.

"Not at all. I'm dying to read all about the families
and old castles here."

"I'll drop you at the bus stop," Dad offered.

Emma got a bus into town, then another to
Castlebridge at the bus station near Eyre Square.
Soon the bus was out of Galway and on the open
road. There had been a fine drizzle all morning, but
when the sun began to shine Emma could feel her
spirits lifting, and by the time the bus reached
Castlebridge she was in a state of high excitement.
She bought a packet of crisps in a small shop and
asked the assistant the way to Moylough Castle.

"There's no one living there now, is there?" she
asked.

"Not at present. But we've just had great news.
This very rich man—made a stack on building in
England—has bought the castle and estate. He's

going to restore it as a luxury hotel and leisure center. So we'll still have our woods."

"What's his name?"

"Something O'Flaherty—I think it's Hugh. He's a multimillionaire, flies around in a helicopter, wants to have a base here in Ireland, says his people came from these parts. And why wouldn't they? The O'Flahertys belong to Connemara."

So O'Flaherty had come home. Maybe a grandson or some relative of his had emigrated to England and started as a builder's laborer, and then his son, and each succeeding generation rose a little higher until at last the O'Flahertys got to the top. And why wouldn't they return to the land of their forefathers and the castle they had once owned?

The sun was still shining as she left the shop and walked to the end of the village, sniffing again the sweet scent of honeysuckle from the hedges and stopping to admire the clumps of foxglove in the ditches.

The road rose steeply with woods on either side, and at the top she paused, remembering how she'd stood there with Sally and Maria and gotten her first glimpse of Moylough Castle. The castle gates were closed, and as she looked into the park with its lime trees, she wondered if they were the same trees she'd seen so long ago. She walked along the crumbling demesne wall and soon came to a place that was low enough to climb over. She stood for a moment trying to get her bearings. Then as she tried to move forward her way was blocked by a thick growth of nettles and brambles. Eventually, with hands scratched from brambles and a white weal from a nettle sting, she had to admit defeat and go back to the road. Then she remembered the back avenue and wondered if she could find it.

Farther on she stopped to ask a farmer who was coming toward her driving three large black and white cows, "Is the back avenue to the castle far from here?"

"Only about another fifty yards or so. But it's all overgrown. Nobody uses it much." The farmer was looking at her curiously.

"Oh, that's all right. I just wanted to know where it was. Thanks," said Emma with a cheerful wave.

The entrance was so overgrown that she almost missed it, but she squeezed her way though and walked up the rough track, almost crying with relief when she saw the gate pillars ahead. She stood with her back against them for a moment before going into the wood, trying to find the path that led to the oak tree.

A startled rabbit scurried for cover as she passed, and birds fluttered in alarm above her as twigs snapped beneath her hurrying feet. And then suddenly there it was, the burr, much bigger now, still on the side of the tree. Reaching for the branch above, she pulled herself up and groped in the hollow trunk. Her hand closed around a circular object and, removing it from

its hiding place, she climbed down and sat beneath the tree to take a closer look.

She was holding a small round box, decorated with flowers. When she lifted the lid, which was cracked and chipped in places, her eyes lit up. Inside was a brooch, modeled in the shape of a butterfly, with tiny rubies and diamonds on its wings.

As she sat there under the oak tree, eyes half closed, she could feel Sally and Maria close to her as she remembered with a smile all their meetings under the oak's spreading branches so long ago.

Yvonne MacGrory was born and raised in County Donegal, in the northwest of Ireland. She is a registered nurse and lives in the town of Kilraine, County Donegal, with her husband, Eamon, and their three children, Jane, Donna, and Mark.

IF YOU ENJOYED THIS BOOK, YOU'LL ALSO WANT TO
READ THESE OTHER MILKWEED NOVELS.

*To order books or for more information, contact Milkweed at
(800) 520-6455 or visit our website (www.milkweed.org).*

THE $66 SUMMER
by John Armistead

MILKWEED PRIZE FOR CHILDREN'S LITERATURE • NEW YORK PUBLIC LIBRARY BEST
BOOKS OF THE YEAR: "BOOKS FOR THE TEEN AGE"

By working at his grandmother's general store in Obadiah,
Alabama, during the summer of 1955, George Harrington
figures he can save enough money to buy the motorcycle he
wants, a Harley-Davidson. Spending his off-hours with two
friends, Esther Garrison, fourteen, and Esther's younger
brother, Bennett, the unusual trio in 1950s Alabama—
George is white, and Esther and Bennett are black—embark
on a summer of adventure that turns serious when they
begin to uncover the truth about the racism in their midst.

GILDAEN, THE HEROIC ADVENTURES OF A MOST
UNUSUAL RABBIT
by Emilie Buchwald

CHICAGO TRIBUNE BOOK FESTIVAL AWARD, BEST BOOK FOR AGES 9–12

Gildaen is befriended by a mysterious being who has lost his
memory but not the ability to change shape at will. Together
they accept the perilous task of thwarting the evil sorcerer,
Grimald, in this tale of magic, villainy, and heroism.

THE OCEAN WITHIN
by V. M. Caldwell

MILKWEED PRIZE FOR CHILDREN'S LITERATURE

Elizabeth is a foster child who has just been placed with the boisterous and affectionate Sheridans, a family that wants to adopt her. Used to having to look out for herself, however, Elizabeth is reluctant to open up to them. During a summer spent by the ocean with the eight Sheridan children and their grandmother, who Elizabeth dubs "Iron Woman" because of her strict discipline, Elizabeth learns what it means—and how much she must risk—to become a permanent member of a loving family.

TIDES
by V. M. Caldwell

Recently adopted twelve-year-old Elizabeth Sheridan is looking forward to spending the summer at Grandma's oceanside home. But on her stay there, she faces problems involving her cousins, five-year-old Petey and eighteen-year-old Adam, that cause her to question whether the family will hold together. As she and Grandma help each other through troubling times, Elizabeth comes to see that she has become an important member of the family.

PARENTS WANTED
by George Harrar

MILKWEED PRIZE FOR CHILDREN'S LITERATURE

After five "adoption parties" and no luck, Andy Fleck, the kid nobody wanted, faces his biggest challenge yet—learning how to live with parents who seem to love him. Placed in a new foster home with Jeff and Laurie, he has a chance to get out of the grip of his past, which includes a jailed father and a mother who gave him up to the state. But Andy can't keep himself from challenging every limit that his foster parents set. So far, Laurie and Jeff have refused to give up on their difficult new charge. But will he go too far?

No Place
by Kay Haugaard

Arturo Morales and his fellow sixth-grade classmates decide to improve their neighborhood and their lives by building a park in their otherwise concrete, inner-city Los Angeles barrio. The kids are challenged by their teachers to figure out what it would take to transform the neighborhood junkyard into a clean, safe place for children to play. Despite their parents' skepticism and the threat of street gangs, Arturo and his classmates struggle to prove that the actions of individuals— even kids—can make a difference.

The Monkey Thief
by Aileen Kilgore Henderson

NEW YORK PUBLIC LIBRARY BEST BOOKS OF THE YEAR: "BOOKS FOR THE TEEN AGE"

Twelve-year-old Steve Hanson is sent to Costa Rica for eight months to live with his uncle. There he discovers a world completely unlike anything he can see from the cushions of his couch back home, a world filled with giant trees and insects, mysterious sounds, and the constant companionship of monkeys swinging in the branches overhead. When Steve hatches a plan to capture a monkey for himself, his quest for a pet leads him into dangerous territory. It takes all of Steve's survival skills—and the help of his new friends—to get him out of trouble.

THE SUMMER OF THE BONEPILE MONSTER
by Aileen Kilgore Henderson

MILKWEED PRIZE FOR CHILDREN'S LITERATURE • ALABAMA LIBRARY ASSOCIATION 1996 JUVENILE/YOUNG ADULT AWARD • MAUDE HART LOVELACE AWARD FINALIST

Eleven-year-old Hollis Orr has been sent to spend the summer with Grancy, his father's grandmother, in rural Dolliver, Alabama, while his parents "work things out." As summer begins, Hollis encounters a road called Bonepile Hollow, barred by a gate and a real skull and bones mounted on a board. "Things that go down that road don't ever come back," he is told. Thus begins the mystery that plunges Hollis into real danger.

TREASURE OF PANTHER PEAK
by Aileen Kilgore Henderson

NEW YORK PUBLIC LIBRARY BEST BOOKS OF THE YEAR: "BOOKS FOR THE TEEN AGE"

Twelve-year-old Page Williams begrudgingly accompanies her mother, Ellie, as she flees her abusive husband, Page's father. Together they settle in a fantastic new world—Big Bend National Park, Texas. Wild animals stalk through the park, and the nearby Ghost Mountains are filled with legends of lost treasures. As Page tests her limits by sneaking into forbidden canyons, Ellie struggles to win the trust of other parents. Only through their newfound courage are they able to discover a treasure beyond what they could have imagined.

I Am Lavina Cumming
by Susan Lowell

MOUNTAINS & PLAINS BOOKSELLERS ASSOCIATION AWARD

In 1905, ten-year-old Lavina is sent from her home on the Bosque Ranch in Arizona Territory to live with her aunt in the city of Santa Cruz, California. Armed with the Cumming family motto, "courage," Lavina deals with a new school, homesickness, a very spoiled cousin, an earthquake, and a big decision about her future.

The Boy with Paper Wings
by Susan Lowell

Confined to bed with a viral fever, eleven-year-old Paul sails a paper airplane into his closet and propels himself into mysterious and dangerous realms in this exciting and fantastical adventure. Paul finds himself trapped in the military diorama on his closet floor, out to stop the evil commander, KRON. Armed only with paper and the knowledge of how to fold it, Paul uses his imagination and courage to find his way out of dilemmas and disasters.

The Secret of the Ruby Ring
by Yvonne MacGrory

WINNER OF IRELAND'S BISTO "BOOK OF THE YEAR" AWARD

Lucy gets a very special birthday present, a star ruby ring, from her grandmother and finds herself transported to Langley Castle in the Ireland of 1885. At first, she is intrigued by castle life, in which she is the lowliest servant, until she loses the ruby ring and her only way home.

A Bride for Anna's Papa
by Isabel R. Marvin

MILKWEED PRIZE FOR CHILDREN'S LITERATURE

Life on Minnesota's Iron Range in 1907 is not easy for
thirteen-year-old Anna Kallio. Her mother's death has left
Anna to take care of the house, her young brother, and her
father, a blacksmith in the dangerous iron mines. So she and
her brother plot to find their father a new wife, even attempt-
ing to arrange a match with one of the "mail order" brides
arriving from Finland.

Minnie
by Annie M. G. Schmidt

WINNER OF THE NETHERLANDS' SILVER PENCIL PRIZE AS ONE OF THE BEST BOOKS
OF THE YEAR

Miss Minnie is a cat. Or rather, she *was* a cat. She is now
a human, and she's not at all happy to be one. As Minnie
tries to find and reverse the cause of her transformation, she
brings her reporter friend, Mr. Tibbs, news from the cats'
gossip hotline—including revealing information that one of
the town's most prominent citizens is not the animal lover
he appears to be.

The Dog with Golden Eyes
by Frances Wilbur

MILKWEED PRIZE FOR CHILDREN'S LITERATURE • TEXAS LONE STAR READING LIST

Many girls dream of owning a dog of their own, but Cassie's
wish for one takes an unexpected turn in this contemporary
tale of friendship and growing up. Thirteen-year-old Cassie
is lonely, bored, and feeling friendless when a large, beautiful

dog appears one day in her suburban backyard. Cassie wants to adopt the dog, but as she learns more about him, she realizes that she is, in fact, caring for a full-grown Arctic wolf. As she attempts to protect the wolf from urban dangers, Cassie discovers that she possesses strengths and resources she never imagined.

BEHIND THE BEDROOM WALL
by Laura E. Williams

MILKWEED PRIZE FOR CHILDREN'S LITERATURE • NEW YORK PUBLIC LIBRARY BEST BOOKS OF THE YEAR: "BOOKS FOR THE TEEN AGE" • MAUDE HART LOVELACE AWARD FINALIST • SUNSHINE STATE YOUNG READER'S AWARD MASTER LIST • JANE ADDAMS PEACE AWARD HONOR BOOK

It is 1942. Thirteen-year-old Korinna Rehme is an active member of her local *Jungmädel,* a Nazi youth group, along with many of her friends. Korinna's parents, however, secretly are members of an underground group providing a means of escape to the Jews of their city and are, in fact, hiding a refugee family behind the wall of Korinna's bedroom. As Korinna comes to know the family, especially their young daughter, her sympathies begin to turn. But when someone tips off the Gestapo, loyalties are put to the test and Korinna must decide in what she believes and whom she trusts.

THE SPIDER'S WEB
by Laura E. Williams

Thirteen-year-old Lexi Jordan has just joined the Pack, a group of neo-Nazi skinheads, as a substitute for the family she wishes she had. After she and the Pack spray paint a synagogue, Lexi hides from her pursuers on the front porch of elderly Ursula Zeidler's home, a former member of the

Hitler Youth Group, who painfully recalls her ugly anti-Semitic Nazi activities and betrayal of a friend that she bitterly rues. When her younger sister becomes enthralled with Lexi's new "family," Lexi realizes the true meaning of the Pack and has little time to save herself and her sister from its sinister grip.

Milkweed Editions publishes with the intention of making a humane impact on society, in the belief that literature is a transformative art uniquely able to convey the essential experiences of the human heart and spirit.

To that end, Milkweed publishes distinctive voices of literary merit in handsomely designed, visually dynamic books, exploring the ethical, cultural, and esthetic issues that free societies need continually to address.

Milkweed Editions is a not-for-profit press.

Join Us

Since its genesis as *Milkweed Chronicle* in 1979, Milkweed has helped hundreds of emerging writers reach their readers. Thanks to the generosity of foundations and of individuals like you, Milkweed Editions is able to continue its nonprofit mission of publishing books chosen on the basis of literary merit—of how they impact the human heart and spirit—rather than on how they impact the bottom line. That's a miracle that our readers have made possible.

In addition to purchasing Milkweed books, you can join the growing community of Milkweed supporters. Individual contributions of any amount are both meaningful and welcome. Contact us for a Milkweed catalog or log on to www.milkweed.org and click on "About Milkweed," then "Why Join Milkweed," to find out about our donor program, or simply call (800) 520-6455 and ask about becoming one of Milkweed's contributors. As a nonprofit press, Milkweed belongs to you, the community. Milkweed's board, its staff, and especially the authors whose careers you help launch thank you for reading our books and supporting our mission in any way you can.

Typeset in Plantin 11/15.5
by Stanton Publication Services.
Printed on acid-free 55# Sebago Antique 2000 paper
by Maple-Vail Book Manufacturing.